Take Me to Side Lake

Jennifer Walters

Barbra June Publishing

For Jessica and Tom Stahl

Also by Jennifer Walters

<u>The Turtle Creek Series</u>

The Memories We Keep

A Side Lake Summer

Return to Side Lake

Christmas in Side Lake

Take me to Side Lake

<u>The Fredrickson's Series</u>

Always Right Here

Northern Winds

Greenrock Road

<u>Standalone</u>

The Weight of Change

www.JenniferWaltersAuthor.com

Brief Character Overview from the Series

The Memories We Keep-Maddy + Brad +Tim

A Side Lake Summer-Lyndsey + Kevin +Tracey

Return to Side Lake- Kat + Ethan +Andy

Christmas in Side Lake- Victoria + Troy

Chapter 1

Lizzy

"All that hard work paid off. How does it feel?"

I pursed my lips together and looked at the menu again, even though I always ordered the same thing every time I was at Bimbos. "It feels like I'm so close, but not quite there."

Troy reached across the table to squeeze my hand. "You're going to pass your boards. The hard part is over. It's a test of all the knowledge you already have stored in that brain of yours."

Emma, our waitress, made her way to our table. "Congratulations, Lizzy! My mom said you were graduating today." She looked at Troy, then back at me again. "I take it the two of you are out celebrating?"

"That's right. Nothing like pizza and wings to celebrate two very long, tough years," Troy said.

He was beaming with pride, and I knew I should feel so much happiness. All the late nights studying, having no social life, never having time for my family.

"I can't even imagine. I don't remember the last time I saw you out in Side Lake. I hope you'll be around to go boating and hang out with us this summer," Emma said. "Are you planning on working?"

"I'm taking my boards next week and if I pass, I should be available until I find a full-time nursing job. I'm working as a CNA right now on the hospital's maternity floor. If I pass my boards, then I'm hoping to secure an RN position."

"On the maternity floor?"

I nodded.

"I love babies. I just don't think I could stand all the blood and bodily fluids and..." Emma shivered. "Anyway, I should probably stop talking about bodily fluids in a restaurant where I make my money selling food, huh?"

I laughed and shook my head. The thought of my boards had my stomach in knots all week. It felt good to laugh and not think about it for a few minutes.

"What can I get for you guys?" She tapped her chin. "Let me guess a pizza, a large George's Special, hot wings, and a pitcher of beer?"

"No beer for..." I was so used to staying away from alcohol to make sure I was getting enough sleep and staying healthy these past two years, I was definitely due for a drink or two. "On second thought, beer sounds great."

Troy nodded, his smile extending to his eyes.

She turned and walked away, and my gaze met Troy's.

"Your aunt would be so proud of you. I'm so proud of you."

To think when I moved in with Troy and my Aunt Victoria, he seemed so cold, and now he was the person I wanted to call every time I got an A or something good happened in my life. He had become a father to me over these past two years.

When Troy said he was proud of me, it sent a shock

straight to my heart. I was proud of where I came from and where I was now.

After Victoria died a little over two years ago, I debated not going to nursing school. I wanted to be there for Troy. His heart was broken, and he needed help running his coffee shop and bookstore, but he set me up in a garage apartment in the town of Virginia, so I was close to the school.

At first, I struggled with being away from Troy and all of his and Victoria's friends, who I had become so close to before Victoria died. But I put my head in my books and soon months had gone by and I had not visited Side Lake. Oh, I visited every big holiday and Troy came to see me every couple of months for dinner, but the pain I felt when I was at Troy's house made me sick to my stomach. The beautiful home my aunt and uncle shared was like a dark shadow that took away all the light. Troy smiled less and spent more time than he should at home. I was glad he had the coffee shop and bookstore to distract him, but seeing him was a reminder that I abandoned him when he needed me the most.

Selfish, I know, but I couldn't help it. I hated being in this house and I dreaded going to Side Lake because of all the memories of my aunt. Being there reminded me of all I lost when she passed away, of watching her deteriorate before my eyes when the cancer took her. First my father, then my aunt. It just wasn't fair.

"Are you okay?" Troy asked, interrupting my thoughts.

I looked away and wiped at the tears under my eyes. "Yeah, it's just hard to take in after all these months that I'm done with school. Once I get my license, I'll be a lot less stressed."

· · ·

Emma came back with the pitcher of beer and set it on the table with two glasses. A waiter came up behind her and put the wings and pizza down on the table, along with two plates.

"Enjoy," Emma said before disappearing into the kitchen.

"How's the coffee shop doing? Is it picking up now that summer is right around the corner?"

He picked up a piece of pizza and touched the cheese before putting it in his mouth. "To be honest, it's been steady since the day we opened it. Sure, it's busier in the spring and summer, but sometimes I don't even get a chance to use the restroom or have time to eat. I can't believe how well it's doing."

I was surprised the store was doing so well, since more than half the cabins and houses on the lake were summer people and not around through the winter months. "Really? That's amazing. I'm so happy for you."

He shrugged. "I never expected it to be so popular, but the kids in college come to do their homework and study. I have a little indoor toddler area so moms can come and let their kids play while they read or have coffee with their friends. And you know coffee. It sells itself."

"That's truly amazing. I guess you're probably going to want my help this summer, huh?"

"Only when you want to. I'm thinking about hiring full-time help this summer so I can spend more time with you and our friends, boating and just relaxing. " He paused. "Right now I just close up when I need to or call my retired teacher friend from Side Lake and she will usually help out."

"Of course. I'll be there as much as I can. You know I love summers in Side Lake."

He did not look convinced. "Lizzy, can I ask you a question?"

My stomach dropped. "Of course."

"Would you consider coming back this summer and staying with me? When you aren't working, of course. I'd love to have you around. My house gets so lonely and I miss you."

I smiled at his question, but I did not want to go back. Not without Victoria. The thought made me want to vomit. "I'll tell you what. I'll move in after my boards. The drive to work isn't too bad. I'd love to be around this summer."

Lies. All lies, but how could I say no? Troy needed me.

His eyes teared up. I could not take my words back now, no matter how much I dreaded living in that house.

"Thank you, Lizzy. We're going to have the best summer. I can't wait to call our friends and let them know."

Oh, great. Now I would have to answer all their questions about where I've been and why I haven't called. What did I get myself into?

"So, you'll come stay with me Memorial weekend then? Everyone is getting together for our annual memorial weekend celebration. We'll get the docks in the water and take the boat out for the first time this year. It'll be fun, I promise."

Was he trying to convince me or himself? His face was thinner than the last time I'd seen him and his broad build was slenderer and the circles under his eyes were darker than I'd ever seen them. He was lonely and still grieving..

As much as I wanted to avoid it, maybe living together would be good for both of us.

Chapter 2

Olivia

The loud knocking kept getting louder and louder until I could no longer ignore it. "Dad, I'll be right back, okay? Someone is at the door."

He nodded and stared blankly at the television while I ran downstairs to answer the door.

"Who is it?" I didn't wait for a reply before I opened the door. "Tim, what are you doing here?" I eyed him curiously.

He ran his fingers through his hair. "I know. I just—"

Mom called out from the kitchen. "Timothy, is that you?" She peeked her head around the corner and hurried over to put her arms around him.

"Tell him to take off his shoes at the door, Liv. Does that boy have no manners?" Dad said from upstairs.

Tim rolled his eyes and took off his shoes.

I shook my head. "Why did you knock? You know you can just come in, right?"

Tim nodded at the door. "The door was locked. I don't mind. I should have called you first to let you know I was coming."

An alarm began going off in the kitchen.

"I have to take dinner out of the oven," Mom said. "You just make yourself comfortable, Timothy." She ran to the kitchen and my father followed her.

Tim put his arm around my shoulders. "Liv, what are you doing here?"

Oh, great. No one told him, and I did not want to talk about it. "Just visiting mom and dad. The real question is, what are you doing here? It isn't like you to just show up. Especially since you still have, what? A week of school left?"

"I live too close to never come around. You live three hours away and here you are. How are you? How's Ben?"

"Good." I lied. I was not ready to have this conversation. The thought of it brought tears to my eyes. I shook them away. "How's Lizzy? I can't believe I haven't met her yet. You've been together for way too long to never bring her around."

He rubbed the back of his neck. Something was wrong, but I could tell he did not want to talk about it.

"She's...ah..."

"Come have some ham and cheese big buns. They're fresh out of the oven. Just in time for company. I'm so glad you came, Tim," Mom said from the kitchen.

Mom was so welcoming and it helped that, unlike me, Tim would not be staying in his old bedroom or asking mom and dad for money. He was the perfect child. A teacher who had not married or got himself tangled up in a loveless marriage.

"I'm starving," Tim said with a pat to his belly.

Two bites into his big bun and Tim opened up his big mouth. "Where's Ben?"

Mom almost choked on her food. Dad raised his

eyebrows at me. They all stopped eating and gave me their full attention.

Awkward silence.

My cheeks got hot.

"Ben and I are not together anymore." I looked down at my food, unable to look him in the eye. He loved Ben. Since Tim moved up north, they had not been in contact that much, but even though I had been with Ben for ten years, I was pretty sure Ben and my brother had more in common than Ben and I did.

"What happened? I thought you guys were so happy. I was expecting a baby announcement, not an announcement like this. Can't you work it out?"

Typical Tim question. "No, Tim. We're divorced and have been for a couple of weeks now."

Tim stopped chewing and stared at me with a hurt expression. He turned to our parents with a questioning look. "Wait, you guys knew, and no one told me?" He wiped his lips with his napkin and scowled at me.

"Why don't you help me with the laundry?" my mother said to my father.

He gave her a confused look, but she grabbed his arm and pulled him out of his chair and into the other room before he questioned her.

"Liv, what happened? Why am I the last to know?"

I took a drink of water to give myself a minute to calm down and answer him without hurting his feelings. "We haven't been happy in years."

He looked at me as if I just told him his pet died. "Really?"

"I know the two of you were close, so this must be hard for you to hear, but that's why I never told you. I didn't have the heart. You were so happy up there in Hibbing."

"Side Lake," he said, interrupting me.

"Whatever. Over in the middle of nowhere by the Canadian border."

"I'm like two hours from the border." He shook his head. "It doesn't matter. Tell me about you and Ben."

"My whole life I've wanted to have children, and I thought Ben did too, but—"

"But?"

"But I found out I was pregnant, and Ben lost it. He said we weren't financially ready and then he admitted he had accepted a job in London, and he wasn't staying."

Tim stood up. "You have to be kidding me? You're pregnant and Ben left you?"

"It's not like that, Tim. We haven't been happy in so long. I was mad at first, too, but then I realized there was no ache in my heart when he told me about London. Sure, I'm sad for our baby, but I don't want to keep living an unhappy life."

My words finally registered in his brain. He looked down at my stomach, then back up at my face. "I can't believe you're pregnant, Liv. I'm so happy for you, but I can't believe Ben would do this."

"Stop blaming him. It is what it is. I wouldn't want my baby growing up in an unhappy home or believing an unhappy marriage and settling is the best way to live. We'll make it work. He's okay with seeing the baby once or twice a year. He's not a complete jerk," I said with a small smile.

"Do you have the house?"

I shook my head. "We sold it in the divorce."

"Where are you living?"

I pursed my lips and looked around me.

His eyes bulged. "You're living with mom and dad?"

I nodded. When he said it like that, I felt like a failure.

"You can't stay here, Liv."

I picked up my plate and took it to the sink to avoid looking at him. "I have nowhere else to go."

He walked up behind me and put his hand on my shoulder. "Yes, you do. Move in with me."

I turned around. "What?" Was he being serious? Me in a small rural town? "Are you serious?"

"I love kids. Let me help you until you get on your feet. You can spend the summer at the lake, relaxing and having some time to yourself before the baby is born and when you're ready to get a job, I can help babysit."

"It's not that easy."

"Liv, you're a nurse. You could work afternoons or midnights and I work day shifts. It's perfect."

"But there's nothing to do up north."

"There's so much to do. We have woods and water and calmness. You don't know what it is like to live in the woods with nature all around you. Side Lake is a lake town with five lakes all connected by channels. It's so peaceful and we can hang out, drive around the lakes in the boat, go hiking, kayaking, whatever you feel like. You'll love the restaurants and especially the people there. Just promise me you'll think about it."

My eyes watered at how much he cared. He really wanted me to come with him.

"Say it," he said.

"I'll think about it."

"That's all I'm asking. Let me be there for you. You don't want to live with mom and dad. Do you?"

I raised my eyebrows at the thought. He knew that was the last thing I wanted. Once you move out of your parent's house, it was so hard to go back. Maybe Tim was right. "Okay. I'll come. I can't promise I'll stay very long but I would love to live with you for a bit and meet all your friends you keep telling me about."

He put his arm around me and kissed the top of my head. "They're going to love you."

He dropped his arm.

"Wait, are you living with anyone?"

"Nope."

"Seeing anyone?"

"Nope."

"I don't think I've ever seen you single, Tim. You really aren't seeing anyone? What happened to Lizzy?"

He chewed on his lip. "It just didn't work out. I don't want to get into it right now."

"I'm so sorry to hear that. I really wanted to meet her."

"Now, you need to come for the summer at least. Not just for a few weeks.."

Did I want to make that much of a commitment? "Why do you want me to come so bad?"

"Because you will be depressed here. Mom and dad are a lot. You want mom lecturing you every time you don't eat healthy or aren't exercising enough? You would be miserable."

He knew exactly how to get me to say yes. "Fine, I'll give it the summer."

He smiled. "I had a feeling you'd say that."

I pointed my finger at him. "But if I don't like it there you won't pressure me to stay. Promise me, Tim. I know you."

"Fine. I promise."

Chapter 3

Lizzy

The sun was warm, but the air had a chill to it. Spring in Minnesota was muddy, sometimes cold, sometimes warm, and always unpredictable. But the wind coming off the lake in Side Lake was refreshing and replenishing. My thoughts shifted to my Aunt Victoria. If she were still alive, she would run out the door right now to greet me. She would fuss over me and make me catch up on everything going on in my life. She had a way of getting me to open up, and she always made me feel comfortable.

"Come inside," Uncle Troy said. "Your room is just the same as you left it. I want to show you something."

I followed him into the house. The minute the door shut behind me, my heart started pounding in my chest. I struggled not to turn around and run out the door. How had it been two years already?

"In here," he said, waving me to follow him downstairs. A sob slipped through my lips at the sight of the basement. He had installed new blue carpet and an indoor movie theater with surround sound. A wedding picture of the two of them with the bright blue lake behind them and the sun beaming down on them sat on a side table. They looked so happy. My heart instantly hurt.

"I always wanted an indoor theater. Victoria told me I was crazy, but I decided why not? I love movies and I thought it would be perfect in the winter when it's too cold to go outside, or even in the summer on a rainy day when we all want to hang out together and it's too cold outside. What do you think?"

This was how he was grieving. He was doing something he always wanted. How was he so strong? How did he have the energy after running the store all day?

The white walls were now dark, and the large projector screen took up most of the far wall. The specialized lighting lit up the room to enhance the cinematic ambiance. The floor had a sectional soft couch and comfortable looking recliners.

He dimmed the lighting for me.

"I can't believe you did all this. Did you hire out a company? It's stunning, Uncle Troy. Absolutely stunning."

He beamed from ear to ear. "I did it myself. I had a little help from the boys, but I picked it all out and delegated. You really like it?"

"The boys, huh?" He was referring to our friends from Side Lake. They were always together, and I was so glad Troy had good friends to lean on when my aunt passed and I moved out. Most of them lived on the same street, which was convenient.

I thought he was miserable and still struggling to get out of bed while he was really at home renovating the basement. Sure, I'd graduated with my nursing degree, but I spent so much time depressed, eating junk food, and crying over losing my favorite person. I threw so much away because I stopped feeling and here he was, fulfilling a dream.

"I can't believe it." I paused, trying to hold back the tears. "I have been so worried about you and so scared to come back here in fear that it would just be too sad for me and...well...I'm so proud of you."

He pulled me in for a side hug and his eyes were watering, too.

"It hasn't been easy, and I miss her so much. But one day I woke up and stopped feeling sorry for myself. I knew your aunt would kill me if she saw me moping around. I wanted to do something. Something I could be proud of. I love the store, but our basement needed some cosmetic surgery. He looked at me and lifted his eyebrows. "You really like it?"

"Yes, I really like it. Now, let's put in a movie. This is exceptional."

"Have a seat."

He beamed as he set up the movie and we both sat down to watch. We put in *Cash for Gold*, which was filmed just twenty minutes away in Chisholm. It wasn't every day we saw a movie filmed in the area. The acting was amazing, and it was so much fun to watch the local businesses and scenery I'd become familiar with in the last few years.

When the movie was over, I looked over at Troy. Tears were running down his face. He covered his face to hide them.

I put my hand on his. "It's okay to cry, you know. No one ever expected you to stop thinking of her."

"I know. It's just lonely sometimes. She was always full of so much life. Remember that time she made us climb the fire tower?"

I shook my head. "How could I forget? She guilted us

into it, and even though not all of us were on board once we climbed to the top, the view was magnificent. Who knew Side Lake could be so beautiful? I could imagine what it looks like in the summer from way up there."

"That's a goal."

"What?"

"We should climb it this summer. Get everyone together to relive that day. What do you think? Too dreary?"

"Absolutely not. They'd love it." I looked down at my watch. "Speaking about the gang, shouldn't we be getting to a bonfire or something?"

"Absolutely," he said. "How did you know we'd be having a bonfire?"

I laughed. "There's always a bonfire."

"This day flew by. It's so great to have you home."

Home? I was afraid he would feel that way. I hated leaving him here all alone. Sure, we had many friends who lived on this street, but this enormous house was empty. "Hey Troy?"

He stretched and yawned. "Hmm?"

"Have you ever thought about dating again?"

His face changed to confusion, maybe even anger. "I can't, Lizzy. I can't do that to Victoria. I'd feel like I was betraying her somehow."

"I know you love her, and you will never forget her, but she'd want you to be happy."

He turned away, angrier than I'd ever seen him. "No. I couldn't. Why would you say that?"

"She'll always be the love of your life, but it's okay to find another person to spend your life with."

In a split second, he was in my face. His face turned red and although I knew he'd never hit me, it seemed like he wanted to. "Don't say that. Don't say another word about it. How could you?"

I put my hands up in surrender. "Okay, I won't say another word about it. Promise."

He relaxed. "I'm sorry. I didn't mean to overreact."

"No, I'm sorry. I just wanted you to know that if you ever meet someone else, I will support you one hundred percent. I told Victoria I would nudge you if you were being stubborn, and you are, but that's okay. You aren't ready, I get it."

My body was still tense. Had I gone too far again? I didn't want to make him angry, but I also wanted him to know he didn't need to choose a life of unhappiness. I wanted him to know he had my blessing.

Troy avoided looking at me when he said, "Why don't you grab a bottle of wine from the wine cellar and I'll get some beer?"

Nothing like avoidance in textbook form.

"I can do that. Meet you upstairs?"

He did not respond, but made his way up the stairs as if I were chasing him.

By the time I got upstairs, Troy was nowhere around. My phone dinged in my pocket. Go figure, a text from Troy.

Uncle Troy: Go ahead and take the wine over there. I'll be there in a few.

He was pissed, but I did not regret suggesting he consider dating. It needed to be said. Maybe he would start thinking about the future now.

I made my way across the road and walked up Kat's

sidewalk. Then I saw him and a gasp slipped out. Tim was walking toward the fire.

How was I able to go months without seeing him and keep him blocked out of my brain, but the first time I ran into him, my heart felt like it would beat out of my chest like a teenager in love? I was sure he did not know I was behind him, so I kept walking as quietly as I could.

His hair had grown a little, and his shoulders looked even broader since the last time I saw him.

Did he have a new girlfriend now? Was she here? I debated running back to Troy's house, but I knew I'd have to see him, eventually. Damn me for telling Troy I'd stay at Side Lake for the summer. I made the wrong choice. I never should have agreed to come back. I was nowhere near ready to see him.

"Lizzy!" Maddy said. "I'm so glad you made it!"

Tim turned around, a surprised look on his face.

Kat and Lyndsey squealed. "Lizzy!"

They wrapped me up in a big hug, and my nerves instantly faded. I squeezed them both tighter, the tears of happiness in full flow.

"Troy said you are spending the summer here! I'm so excited. Please stay with me whenever you want. I've missed you so much," Kat said.

Once we broke apart, Lyndsey took the wine from me, corked it open, and pulled out the travel wine glasses.

"Troy's wine cellar, great choice on the Cabernet," Kat said.

"Congratulations, Nurse Lizzy," Kevin said with a fist bump.

Ethan walked over and hugged me tight. "We're so damn proud of you."

"Victoria always knew you'd do it," Maddy said.

I had to change the subject quick, or I would start crying. "So, what's new with all of you? I heard you boys helped Troy with the home theater? It looks unbelievable."

"A theater? You have to be kidding me," Lyndsey said in disbelief. She glared at Kevin and Ethan. "You guys knew about this."

"We helped," Kevin said.

Ethan snorted. "What? Troy and I did most of the work. Kevin worked on drinking the beer and testing the new popcorn maker."

"I can't believe you guys didn't tell me you were building a theater in Troy's basement. I want to see it," Kat said.

My eyes landed on Tim's.

He responded with a small smile, and in response, a hot flush rode up my traitorous neck. This was not happening. It wasn't. I no longer wanted to be with him, but my feelings would not stop me from enjoying the scenery.

Kevin stepped forward. "Now, where the heck is Troy?"

Chapter 4

Olivia

I heard their voices, but I was not ready to meet a bunch of new people, so I made my way down the road instead. A weird sound in the woods stopped me in my tracks. Was it a deer? A bunny? A squirrel maybe? Was it chirping?

Curious, I cautiously made my way toward the noise in the trees across the street. Was I trespassing on someone's property? Great, I would probably get arrested or shot or something. After all, I was in hunting territory. Didn't everyone have guns?

When I got closer to the noise, I peeked through the pine trees and saw what looked to be a grown man sitting on a stump. What was he doing?

I squinted to get a better look. He slowly rose and raised his arm. His elbow cocked back, then sprung forward. Was he...target shooting?

He lowered his bow and shook his head.

I moved closer to get a better view of the target without him noticing me and stepped on a tree branch with a loud pop.

His head turned around so fast, I wasn't sure who was more startled

He walked toward me. "Hello?"

I covered my face and closed my eyes tight behind them.

"Hello? The store is closed for the night. You can come back tomorrow at ten. And by the way, I can see you standing there even if you are covering your eyes."

The store? Was there a store out here? What was he talking about? I took it as my cue to turn around and walk away. How embarrassing to be spotted spying on this man. What an impression I was making in this small town where everyone probably knew everyone.

I turned around to leave, but glanced back. He turned his head to follow my gaze at the tree behind the target. He looked back at me again, eyeing me curiously.

I let out a small laugh and covered my mouth.

"My hand slipped," he said in a defensive tone.

"I didn't say anything."

"But you wanted to."

I took a step in the opposite direction, but then turned back. "It is killing me just a little. I was actually trying to see if maybe you stepped on your glasses or something and that's why your aim was so off."

He shook his head at me. "What's your name, Miss Judgmental?"

"It's Ima. Ima Judgmental. Dad joke." I pursed my lips.

Now it was his turn to chuckle. "Well, Ima. Do you think you can do any better? Be my guest." He extended his arm toward the arrows next to him.

I pulled my sweatshirt over my head. His gaze was focused on my midsection. My tank top had been hooked on my sweatshirt and just a sliver of skin was visible. I pulled down my shirt, cleared my throat, and tied my sweatshirt around my waist. His gaze jerked away fast.

I suspected he was married or in a serious relationship by the guilty look on his face and the blushed cheeks.

I walked up to him as he handed me the bow. I chose an arrow and locked it into place. I put my fingers in the grips and tried to pull back on the strings, but I only made it back an inch before the force was too heavy for my weak arms.

He laughed and took a step toward me.

"Have you ever shot a bow before, Ima?"

"Not since junior high, but I've always wanted to get back into it. I was hoping I'd get a bullseye on my first shot."

He moved closer. I felt the heat off his chest on my back. He lightly kicked my feet.

"Your feet need to be perpendicular to the target and shoulder length apart."

I did as he said.

"Now turn your toes out slightly."

"It feels uncomfortable."

"It's for more stability." He pushed me gently to prove his point.

"In case someone tries to push me over?"

He shook his head at my stupid comment. "Don't grab the handle like a hammer. Rest the grip against the bony part of your palm's heel." He guided my fingers back into the grips.

A chill ran down my spine. His cold hands were touching my bare skin. The simple, most intimate touch had my heart pounding in my chest. Hopefully, he did not notice.

"Lower your fingers under the shelf and relax your hand."

Huh? Was he speaking in another language? It wouldn't

matter. All I heard was the pounding of my heart deep in my eardrum.

"Make sure to form as straight a line as you can from your grip hand all the way back to your shoulder."

He ran his hand up my arm and sparks ran across my skin from his touch.

"Make sure not to lock your bow arm, but don't bend it too much, either. Now, let's knock an arrow."

I gave him a confused look.

He grabbed the arrow and put it in front of my face. "You need to insert the nock near the middle of the bowstring. This metal piece here will help you aim."

"Got it," I said, my heart still pounding in my chest. Was it from the closeness of his body to mine? The nerves or excitement of shooting a bow? Maybe it was the pine needle man smell that had my senses dancing.

I put the tip end on the handle of the bow.

"Make sure not to rest the arrow in your hand or it will be painful when you let it go."

I breathed in deeply and held it.

He put his fingers on mine again. "Now draw the string back. Your hand needs to rest on your face."

He pulled the bow with me, but it still made my hands and arms shake with the weight.

"Now look down at the shaft of the arrow. It should point at your target."

I was still holding my breath, focusing on not letting go.

"Ready, fire!"

Pain shot through my arm on the inside of my elbow, and I cried out with the shock of it.

"You okay?"

I held my arm and looked at where the arrow landed,

five feet short of my target. "The string came back and stung my arm."

He grabbed my arm and pointed at the red mark. "That would be a zinger."

"No shit, Sherlock. You could have warned me, you know?"

"Women's arms angle out more from the elbow. It isn't an issue for me."

"How convenient," I said playfully. "I better tend my injuries. I'm sorry to say, but your coaching skills are as good as your shots."

"Ouch," he said in a monotone voice and held his chest.

"I wouldn't quit your day job," I said over my shoulder as I walked away, smiling from ear to ear.

That was so much fun, to feel desired and flirting with him. I had no interest in seeing him again or anything since I was pregnant. Soon I'd have a huge belly and swollen ankles, and I couldn't be more excited. A baby was so much better than my loveless marriage or starting over in another relationship. I was going to be a mom, and that made me happy. What was life, really, without children? I placed my hand on my belly. No bump yet, but I knew it was just a matter of time.

I had made the right choice. I knew it in that moment as I found my way to the fire. A summer at the lake was just what I needed, and I was glad I'd told Tim I was staying.

Finding the right house was easy. I followed the laughter and loud voices coming from down the street. Night had not fallen, but the fire was going and a tall man with defined calves, thick arms, and a Twins hat was standing over the grill flipping burgers.

"You made it," Tim said, making his way to me. "Guys, I want you to meet my little sister, Olivia."

I gave a small wave. "Hello."

My social anxiety was in full swing with all the unfamiliar faces. I had no problem talking to people as a nurse, but walking into a social gathering with a bunch of unknown faces staring at me and judging me filled me with paralyzing fear.

I waited for them to say a quick hello and turn away, but instead they all came right up to me with big smiles and open arms.

"Hi, Olivia, I'm Maddy. Your brother and I worked at the school together when he was subbing at Dylan Elementary School in Hibbing."

A man with a grin stepped up from behind Maddy. He put his arm around her waist and kissed her cheek before extending his hand to me. I shook it and surprisingly the moment wasn't awkward. "And I'm her husband Brad. Let's just say your brother and I had our issues when he first moved here, but now he's my buddy."

He grabbed Tim and put him in a headlock. They were obviously very close.

"And this is Kevin. Ethan is over there cooking. That's Kat, and this is Lyndsey." They each said hello, and the women came in for hugs.

"I am so excited to hear you're staying here for the summer. We have killer beach parties, and we spend most of the summer on the beach, in the lake, or boating," Maddy said.

"I think she'll fit in just fine," my brother said. "She loves all those things except she can't ski because—"

I elbowed him in the stomach, and he grunted and held

his breath. I was not ready to tell them I was pregnant. Not yet. I did not know them. "Sorry."

He gave me a look that seemed to say, point taken.

Of all our siblings, I was always the closest to my brother. Sure, he teased me like any brother would, but he was always there for me and he was the kind of guy that would give you the shirt off his back. He also was not someone people messed with.

I saw a cute blonde come out of the house and shut the door behind her. Everyone turned to look.

"And this is Lizzy," Maddy said, smiling at her.

I eyed my brother, and he looked away nervously. "Oh, Lizzy. I've heard so much about you."

Her cheeks blushed, and she gave Tim a confused look, but only for a second, as if the eye contact startled her. If I knew my brother, this had to be his fault. He always seemed to ruin any good relationship that came his way. He was labeled a ladies' man because he had that swagger and confidence women swooned over, but they never took him seriously. His relationships never lasted long. He tried to act like he did not care, but I could always see right through his act.

It broke him. Repeatedly.

"Well, it's nice to meet you," she said in a shy voice.

Ethan cleared his throat. "The burgers are ready, dish up."

"And there's Troy. Better late than never," Kevin said.

Troy? The guy with the bow? I looked right at him, and our eyes locked.

"Ima?"

Oops.

Chapter 5

Lizzy

Tim frowned and shook his head. "Ima? Who's Ima? What are you talking about?"

"I'm so sorry. You look like someone I know. I'm Troy," he said, reaching his hand out to Olivia.

Something felt a bit off, and I doubted I was the only one who noticed it. Olivia seemed to be avoiding eye contact with Troy.

"Troy, this is my sister, Liv. She's up from the Cities. She's going to be staying with me this summer," Tim said.

"Oh?" His words sounded more like a question.

"So, what do you do, Liv? Are you planning on working while you're here?" Ethan said.

Kat nudged him. "She doesn't want to work at the B&B, babe."

"I'm a nurse," Olivia said.

Not only had Tim never mentioned more than a few words about his sister, but he never said one word about one of his sisters being a nurse. Why hadn't he introduced us when I was in panic mode about going back to school? How did I ever think we had a chance when he never opened up about his past or his family? I only knew he had five sisters and grew up in Duluth.

Not that it mattered anymore. He was not my boyfriend. That ship had sailed. He was a closed book and even though it still hurt, I could never be in a relationship with someone who could not open up. After my ex-boyfriend, Dalton, I'd never settle again.

Dalton was a controlling, manipulative drug dealer. He secluded me from all my friends and family. I thought he was protecting me. When we were robbed at gunpoint and my life flashed before my eyes, I finally woke up. He was as dangerous as the guys who held us at gunpoint and robbed us. I left him and found my way to Side Lake and back into my Aunt Victoria's home where I had the support to never go back. The last time I saw Dalton, he was being arrested. I was so much stronger now than I was two years ago. That horrid period in my life felt like a lifetime ago. The thought of those days made me ill.

"Now the two of you must already know each other, right?" Kevin said.

I bit my lip.

Olivia punched Tim's arm, "No. My brother's been holding out on me. Today is the first time we've actually met." She side-eyed Tim. "What do you do, Lizzy?"

"I just graduated from nursing school, but I still have to take my boards."

"I'm a nurse, too! Congratulations. If you want any help studying, I'd love to help you. Just say the word." Olivia's entire demeanor transformed within seconds from the bashful girl I saw just moments ago. Her energy and positivity were contagious.

"Yeah, that would be great. Thank you. I'm so nervous."

"Don't be. You'll be fine."

Everyone made their way to the table laden with food. Liv and I lingered behind, still deep in conversation.

"Do you know where you want to work? What specialty are you going into?"

I knew exactly what I wanted. "I'm a CNA at a hospital in Virginia on the maternity floor. I want to stay on the maternity floor and then hopefully end up in pediatrics."

"Kids and babies, I love it. I'm the same way. I've been a nurse for three years working on the maternity floor myself in the Cities. I thought about applying around here if there are any openings, but I don't know how long I'm staying yet."

"Would you ladies like a drink? I have seltzers or boxed wine," Lyndsey said.

"I'm okay right now," Olivia said.

"There's juice and pop inside. Would you like me to get you anything?" Lyndsey said to Olivia.

"Juice sounds good, but please, let me get it. I need to use the restroom, anyway."

"Absolutely. Let me show you where it is."

"I'll show her. I was going inside anyway," Troy said.

I may have imagined it, but Olivia held her breath for a moment before agreeing to follow him inside. They just met, so I had to be imagining it.

My eyes locked with Tim's, and he looked away before I had the chance to do it first. He seemed to be as nervous as I was.

The fire burned bright once the sun set, and pesky mosquitoes were missing since it was still late spring. The night was peaceful and the air light. Laughter filled the air, but I still struggled to breathe with Tim sitting across the fire from me.

An hour later, I snuck away and tried to sneak back to Troy's house without being noticed.

"Lizzy! Wait!"

I knew his voice before I turned around. I wanted to keep walking, but I'd already stopped. "What's up?" I tried to keep my voice calm.

I could see only the outline of his body in the darkness. The light of the moon blocked his perfect features and made me feel less vulnerable in his presence.

"Let me walk you home."

I did not reply, but instead started walking again, this time with Tim by my side.

"You haven't answered my texts."

I laughed under my breath. "When was the last time you texted me, Tim?"

"Fair. I guess it's been a while. Did I do something wrong?"

I was being unfair. I was the one who left him. I was the one who ghosted him. I was the one who walked away. "No. I'm sorry. I'm just exhausted. Can we talk about this another time?"

He sped up and stood in front of me, blocking me, as we reached Troy and Victoria's house.

"No. I'm sorry, Lizzy, but I've waited long enough. I've been patient. I know you weren't ready when I gave you the ring and—"

Fire built in my lungs. "Fine, you want to do this right now? Fine. Let's go inside. You're right. We need to clear the air." He knew how to push my buttons.

"I have a better idea."

He reached down for my hand and led me to the water. "I have a feeling Troy put the canoe out. Want to go for a ride?"

"Now? Really?"

"It's a beautiful night, no bugs, and that canoe looks so lonely. We might as well take it out on the lake."

He stepped off the dock and into the canoe, his body lit up by the bright moon.

He reached his hand out to me, and for some reason, my hand reached out to meet his. He helped me into the canoe. The boat wobbled underneath my feet, causing me to stumble as I moved to the seat and faced him. Once I sat down, I realized I was seated the wrong way but I'm was too unsteady to turn my body around.

He handed me a paddle and pushed us away from the dock. We slowly paddled away, and the darkness swallowed up the canoe. The water was calm, but we stayed near the shoreline.

"Don't worry, we won't go far," he said, reading my mind.

He pulled out a flashlight and clipped it to the back of the canoe. It exploded light from behind him, and I had to shield my eyes.

"This looks like a good spot to stop," he said, setting the paddle down. "I have something I really need to say. It's been eating me up since that... day."

I'd like to say I had to question which day he was referring to, but he and I both knew it needed no further explanation.

He cleared his throat. "I still don't understand what happened. I loved you, Liz."

As the full moon made its way past a cloud, the water lit up around us. He turned around to point the flashlight into the water instead of at us. His hands were as restless as my heart, and I knew he was giving me time to answer.

"I know. When you whipped out that ring and got

down on your knee, it seriously made me so happy. That moment was one of the happiest days in my life, but also the hardest. I knew I wasn't ready. It was too soon."

He nodded. "I understand you weren't ready, but why did you run away? Why did you ghost me?"

"Because your proposal made me realize you didn't know me at all. My aunt had just passed away. I was starting school. I needed some space. I'm sorry I hurt you."

"Hurt me?" He laughed. "Hurt me?" His voice softened. "It broke me."

I crossed my arms. "Take me back to the dock, now."

"I'll take you back after you answer why you ran. Why you're trying to run again? Just talk to me, please."

I grabbed the other paddle. "If you won't take us back, I will."

He held my paddle tight. "Stop, Lizzy. I know you better than anyone else. What did I do to hurt you this bad? Did have something to do with what you went through with Dalton? Was that it?"

"Dalton? You've got to be kidding me. I didn't want to marry you and you don't seem to take no for an answer, just like you're proving right now."

"You've been avoiding me for too long. I've missed you. Talk to me, please."

Fire burned in my chest. "Take it back," I said. "This has nothing to do with him. I don't ever want to hear his name again, okay?"

"Fine," he said. "I'm sorry. I know it has nothing to do with him. But you need to stop running."

"I'm not running. I needed time. Everything that happened was too much. Maybe coming back here for the summer was a mistake."

"You don't mean that," he said. "I still love you, Lizzy. Talk to me."

Desperation was in his voice as he tried to plead with me.

We reached the dock, and I grabbed onto the side to pull the canoe in. I wanted to get out of the boat as quick as I could without stumbling. He was right, I was running away. I did not want him to see that I was still broken, that I could not be happy. I was all alone and the only time I felt alive was when I was at school or working, where I could escape the pain.

The boat shook as I lost my grip and Tim tried to lean over to help, but I was now standing and wobbly. A wave came from out of nowhere and bounced the boat. I fell backward onto Tim's lap. He caught me, but the force of my fall caused him to fall back. He was now on his back on the floor of the canoe and I was on top of him, my back to his chest.

My forehead stung, and when I went to touch it, a bump was forming.

"You okay?"

I couldn't sit up, so I turned over and pushed myself off his chest. "I'm okay, but I must have hit my head. I have a bump."

He helped me back to the seat, then grabbed onto the dock and pulled himself up. I bent my knees to stabilize as he pulled me up onto the dock. "I don't remember canoes being that tippy," I said, feeling the bump on my forehead again. Was it getting bigger?

He took out the flashlight and shined it on my head, his face just inches from mine. His full lips and the way his tongue hung out of his mouth when he was focusing pulled at my heart.

"Look at me," he said, checking my eyes with the flashlight.

"Your pupils look good, but you'll have one heck of a bump on your head."

I pushed away his hand and made my way toward Troy's house.

He grabbed my hand and held it. "I won't keep pushing you, but I miss you, Lizzy. Please don't hide from me anymore. I love you."

I nodded. "Just let it go, okay?"

A look of disappointment etched across his face. "I won't mention it again."

Chapter 6

Olivia

Troy led me into the empty kitchen and grabbed the cranberry juice, lifting it to get my approval. I nodded back.

"No drinking for you tonight, huh?"

"Nah. I just met these people. I'm not ready to get all drunk and make a fool out of myself yet." I was never much of a drinker even before I was pregnant.

"So what's your story?"

"Excuse me?" I nervously wrapped my finger around my brown curls and twirled them.

"Your story. What brings you to Side Lake other than your brother?"

"You think I need a reason to spend a summer with my brother?"

He raised his eyebrows.

"Okay, fine. I'm going through some stuff. My husband and I recently got divorced."

He dropped his head. "I'm sorry to hear that." His jaw clenched. "That's terrible."

I waved him off. "Yeah, it's hard, but it's good. We

wanted different things out of life. I was too young and settled with a guy that was perfect on paper, but not really for me."

His eyes never left mine.

"I don't want to bore you with the details and ruin a good night. It was bound to happen, eventually."

He poured himself a glass of water, his back now to me, which made it easier for me to speak. "What's your story?"

His arm lifted as he gulped down the glass of water. "I've never been through a divorce, but I've been married."

So he wasn't hitting on me. He was happily married. That explained why he seemed so nervous when he spoke to me. "Oh. Kids?"

I stepped in front of him. His eyes looked so sad, and his lip quivered.

"Oh no, did something happen to your kid?" My heart raced at the thought. It was none of my business, but he looked so sad. "You don't have to answer that. That was so insensitive of me."

He shook his head again and flashed a warm smile. "Nope. Never had any kids. We wanted to have kids but—but she was taken too soon."

I moved closer and clasped his arm gently. "I'm so sorry, Troy. Your wife? She..."

I did not need to finish that thought to know I was right. He lost his wife. He put his fist in front of his mouth and took a deep breath to halt his emotions. He finally nodded, but tears shone in his eyes and made me want to wrap him in a giant hug. But since we just met, I felt that would be a little inappropriate. "When?" After the question slipped out of my mouth, I tried to take it back, but he answered.

"A little over two years ago. Cancer."

"I'm so sorry."

"I rarely tell people the first day I meet them, but you seem so trusting. Are you sure you aren't a therapist?"

I laughed. "Nope. Not that I know of. I'm glad you shared it with me, though. But I feel like a jerk for going on about my divorce when you're dealing with something so tragic."

He put his hands in his pockets. "Don't be. A divorce is a big deal. I'm sorry you went through it. I'm sure you're just as broken as I am under all that strong skin of yours."

I was guarded and had yet to break down. How could I, when I had had second thoughts from the day my husband proposed? The mistake was mine. But my clock was ticking, and I was sick of all the questions from my parents about when we were going to get pregnant, so I settled.

"What broke me was living with my parents after we split. My parents are great, don't get me wrong, but I felt like a failure. When Tim found out and talked me into staying at the lake for a few months, I felt worse, but then I realized it wasn't charity. He really wanted me to stay with him. Because he cared."

"You guys are close?"

"We used to be. We grew up with four other siblings. All sisters, by the way, but I was always the closest to Tim. I'm a few years older than him. He used to follow me and my friends around all the time when he was little. I was the cool big sister." I smiled at the memory.

"Poor guy. That's a lot of women in one house. A whole lot of estrogen."

I pushed him playfully. "Watch it, buddy."

He put his hands up in surrender.

"How about you? Have any siblings?"

He nodded. "You met Kevin out there. He's my brother."

"The good-looking one built like a brick shit house? That's your brother?"

He patted his belly. "Hey. What are you saying?"

I laughed. "Oh, stop. You're far from overweight. You could probably put on a few pounds."

"Ouch! You calling me skinny now?"

I shook my head.

"He's a cop. He has nothing better to do than lift weights."

Kevin definitely looked like a cop, with his hard eyes and perfect posture. He held himself like he was either a police officer or in the military.

"I'm sure he doesn't sit around the police station all day lifting weights. No one gives the police enough credit for what they do, if you ask me."

"Agreed," he said. "I wouldn't dare mess with my brother. Don't tell him I said that. I'd never hear the end of it."

We made our way back outside, though neither one of us wanted to end our conversation. He was so easy to talk to.

The fire was still burning strong when we reached the beach. Everyone seemed a bit more intoxicated than when we left, but I was not complaining. No one was alert enough to ask us questions about our disappearance.

I looked around for Tim, but he was missing. So was Lizzy. "Have you seen my brother?" I said to Maddy.

She glanced around the fire and wrinkled her forehead. "I saw him sneak off quite a while ago. I hope he didn't ditch out early."

I leaned in. "Do you think he left with Lizzy?"

She gave me a puzzled look, then her eyes widened. "I sure hope so. I'd love to see those two get back together."

"What happened between the two of them, anyway?" I said.

She leaned in a little closer and looked around to make sure no one was listening. "He doesn't like to talk about it, but I think something happened a couple years ago when she moved out of Side Lake and went to school. Tim moped around for quite a while after that, but every time one of us tried to talk to him, he dismissed it. That happened right after Victoria died, so I'm sure that had something to do with it. Lizzy disappeared from all of us, including Troy."

"Victoria is Troy's wife?"

"Yeah. We were all such a tight group of friends and then Victoria got cancer and it changed everything. When she passed, a part of us seemed to go with her. Last summer was so quiet. Everyone was too busy. Kat and Ethan spent the summer in Europe, and Emma took care of the B&B. Josh and Whitney did their own thing. The group pretty much became Brad, me, Lyndsey, and Kevin. Tim came around here and there and we spent a lot of time helping Troy with his store, but it just wasn't the same."

No wonder Troy was so broken. Victoria obviously made a big impression on everyone.

Troy's words from earlier in the woods circled in my mind. He said something about a store and coming back tomorrow morning when it opened, but I was not sure what he was talking about. I never saw a store on this road now that I thought about it. "Tell me about his store."

"Before Victoria got sick, they planned on opening up a coffee shop, and she always wanted to have a bookstore, so when she passed, Troy added books to the store and dedicated it to her. It's really a beautiful tribute. His store does so well out here all year long, and brings in a lot of businesses for the restaurants, too. He even added a skating rink in the winter out in front of his house on the lake."

"Really? Two great people lucky enough to find each other only to have their marriage end in such a sad way. I can tell he's a really nice guy. And to be honest, I could spy a Cinnamon Roll a mile away.

"Cinnamon Roll?"

I nodded. "It's a trope in romance novels that is a term for a sweet, kind, and supportive man. Selfless. You know, too big for this world."

"I didn't realize that. You're a reader? You'll love all the books at his store then. Just wait until you see all the boats pull up to the dock in front of his store. He promised he would take it easy this summer and hire more help or close it more often so we can spend more time enjoying the lake. We only get a few months of summer, as you know, so we all like to take advantage of the summer when we can."

"Makes sense. It's why you live at the lake, right?"

"Exactly. Now, let's see if we can find Tim."

Chapter 7

Lizzy

I walked in the door to the smell of bacon. "Uncle Troy, what smells so good?"

He opened the oven and pulled out blueberry muffins. "I made a celebratory brunch and invited our friends over to celebrate our favorite nurse."

"Hey, what am I? Chopped liver?" Olivia said behind me.

"Oops," he said. "Didn't see you there, Ima."

He clearly saw her walk in with me and why was he calling her Ima? I was so confused. Before I addressed it, Kevin and Ethan came bursting in the door.

Kevin was holding a stethoscope, and Ethan had a gift bag.

"We come bearing presents!" Ethan said in a singsong voice.

"I love presents," I said, dancing across the floor to hug them.

I wasn't expecting to become so attached to being back in Side Lake. I wanted to get as far away from Tim as possible, but who was I kidding? This was my family, and I forgot how much I missed them and needed them in my life.

The memories of Victoria made my heart ache. It felt wrong being in this house without her. Although I only lived here for a short time, this was the only place that ever felt like home to me.

"You guys are the best. Thank you."

"The nursing boards weren't terrible, were they?" Olivia said.

"Funny," I said. "Real funny. They were so hard. Although, I don't think I could have done it without you. Thank you for helping me prepare."

Olivia had spent the last few days helping me study and preparing me for my boards. I got to know her and I really liked and looked up to her. She was a few years older than I was and definitely more experienced in the nursing field.

We had some time alone to get to know each other. She opened up about her ex-husband, and I told her about Dalton. She avoided bringing up Tim, and I did too.

"I'm glad I could help, but you took that test all on your own. You're going to be a fine RN, Lizzy."

Troy put the food on the table, grabbed six plates, and handed them to me.

Maddy walked through the door with Kat right behind her. "How about mimosas to kick off this brunch?"

"Don't mind my friend here. Whitney took David for the night, so she's kid free."

"Where's Brad and Lyndsey?" Troy said

"They're with their parents helping them with something," Maddy said. "But I skipped out because I couldn't miss our girl becoming a successful nurse after months of studying her butt off."

I could feel my face flush.

Three knocks on the door and Tim stuck his head in. "What did I miss?"

"Lizzy passed the boards," Olivia said. He flashed me the smile he knows I can't resist, his dimple appearing just in time for him to yell out, "Congratulations!"

Everyone stared at us in silence.

Awkward.

Kat eyed the counter. "The true question is, who made the cake? You do have a cake. Don't you?"

Troy reached into the fridge and pulled out an apple pie. "Lizzy would rather have an apple pie, wouldn't you?" He leaned in and whispered, "I used your aunt's secret recipe."

Tears welled up in my eyes. I wanted Aunt Victoria to be here for this moment with me. I called my mom, but although she was sober, she did not understand how important the boards were to me. She was too busy traveling across the country with her new boyfriend. We just weren't as close as we used to be."You made a pie for me?'

His smile widened. "Of course I did. Breakfast bake, muffins, and apple pie." He set the pie down on the counter, then reached into the freezer. "Á la mode?"

"Did you really need to ask me that? You know me better than that."

Troy smiled. "True. I didn't need to ask. Did I?"

"Did you tell her the good news?" Tim said to Olivia.

"Tim," Kat said, nudging him in the side. "I think Olivia wanted to be the one to tell her."

"That's why I said that."

What was it everyone knew except me?

Olivia smiled. "It's not a big deal. I probably should have told you, but I applied to the hospital, and I'll be your new co-worker. I hope that's okay."

In shock was not a big enough word to describe how I felt. My new co-worker? "You got a job in Virginia?"

Olivia bit her lip and shrugged. "I hope that's okay. I wanted it to be a surprise. I hope you aren't mad."

Excitement poured out of me, and I jumped into her arms and squeezed her tight. "You're staying? Really? I'd love that."

She let out a breath of air. "You aren't mad?"

I shook my head. "Why would I be?"

"I don't know. You sure that's okay?"

"I'm absolutely sure. I won't be the only one working this summer. I can't wait to work with you."

Tim stared at us. The confused look on his face made me even happier. I had made the right choice in letting him go. He never felt comfortable enough to introduce me to any of his family when we were together. He obviously did not feel even remotely as into me as I did to him. He knew almost everything about my family. Heck, he knew my aunt and uncle better than I did, yet he told me very little about his family.

"Congrats!" Maddy and Kat said.

I leaned closer to Olivia so she could hear me over the excited voices. "When do you start?"

"Not for a few days."

Tim crossed his arms. "You aren't working Memorial Day? Are you?"

"No, I'm not working Memorial weekend. Don't worry."

Tim wiped his brow. "Oh good. I would be pretty upset if you missed Memorial Day in Side Lake."

Troy cracked open a beer and took a gulp. "There is nothing like summer Side Lake style and Memorial Weekend kicks off summer."

"It's true, just wait until the Fourth of July," I said.

"She's right. This is the best place to spend the Fourth of July. I think we need to make a float and be in the parade this year. What do you guys think?" Maddy said.

She was jumping up and down and clapping with so much excitement, how could we turn her down?

"I'm in," I said. "What should our theme be?"

"How about The Ladies of Turtle Creek, and we can make the theme to market Troy's coffee shop!"

"Yeah, and we can highlight Ethan," Kevin said, squeezing Ethan's shoulder and slapping his chest. "Our famous author of Turtle Creek Road here."

"You mean New York Times bestselling author? Yeah, please, honey? It would be so much fun and it's for a good cause," Kat pleaded. "And Side Lake loves when our famous author makes an appearance in town. You have to!"

"We could hand out bookmarks and candy!" Maddy said. "I get to make up the bookmarks."

"Only if I get to shoot squirt guns at people," Ethan said.

"You know how my guy is," Kat said. "So humble. Doesn't want to draw attention to himself." She leaned her head on his shoulder, and he just shook his head.

"Shooting water at people is a great way to distract everyone," I said. "Although a sea theme could be cute, too."

"Yeah, they probably won't even see it coming," Olivia said.

Ethan smiled. "You're too kind. It's really not a big deal." He turned to Troy. "I do like the idea of promoting your coffee shop, though. I think it would be a magnificent tribute to Victoria. We could even pass out pink ribbons."

Maddy's mouth formed an O. "That's a great idea! Why didn't I think of that?"

"Victoria sounds like such a wonderful person. I wish I could have met her," Olivia said.

"You would have loved her, sis. She was the kindest person in Side Lake," Tim said.

Kat nodded. "Most hospitable person."

"She would have loved you," Tim said. "She also made the best apple pie. Should we see if Troy's compares?"

Uncle Troy turned around to grab the forks and spoons out of the drawer. He turned back toward us, and that's when I saw the tears in his eyes. He blinked them away and smiled when he saw me looking at him. I wanted to give him a hug, but I knew it would only make him more emotional.

Kevin took a fork and stuck it into the pie before Troy had a chance to set it down on the table. The fork made it into his mouth before Kat had a chance to swat his hand away.

He let out a loud moan. "Oh, my gosh. Who knew you could bake like this? Victoria would be so proud."

Olivia's eyes jumped to Troy's, and they locked eyes for just a second longer than normal. I knew it. Sparks were flying. About time. He deserved to be happy and whether they became friends or more, my goal this summer was to make sure they got to know each other.

Chapter 8

Olivia

"Wait up, Olivia," Troy said from behind me. "Do you prefer to go by Olivia or Liv?"

I loved that he cared enough to ask. "Either one."

His cheeks turned pink and he struggled to look directly at me. "I was wondering if maybe you wanted to do some target practice tomorrow or maybe go for a hike with me."

I hesitated and stared at him curiously. "Why do you ask?" He was so fun to mess with.

His eyes scrunched together. "I'd like to hang out. Maybe show you around." He paused. "If you want."

I eyed him with skepticism. "Why?"

He ran his hand through his hair and no longer made eye contact. "I thought since Tim has to work tomorrow, it could be fun. I'd hate for you to sit around and be bored."

I put my hand on my hip. "Are you hitting on me?"

He took a nervous step backward and held out a hand to stop me. "No, I—"

"I'm just kidding," I said with a laugh. But I had gone a bit too far and felt a little bad about it. "Let's go for a hike tomorrow. Sorry, but I can't help embarrassing you. You did call me Ima in front of all your friends."

He opened up his mouth to speak, and I laughed again.

"I'm sorry, you're too easy."

His mouth hung open. I turned around and headed for Tim's house. I looked back and said, "See you at seven in the morning, or is that too early for you?"

He stopped and shook his head. "You better not stand me up."

"I guess you'll find out tomorrow," I said. Teasing Troy was just too easy.

Troy was right on time.

Tim was working, it was the last day of school before Memorial Weekend. A perfect day for me to sneak away without my brother assuming this was more than what it was.

"So, where are we going?" I asked.

"McCarthy Beach State Park."

We drove to the park in a comfortable mutual silence. The silence was peaceful, with no expectations.

Once we drove onto highway five and took a left, Troy turned to me. "This is the perfect time of year to go hiking. No mosquitoes yet, the weather isn't too hot or too cold, and the grass is still short. It makes for a much easier hike."

"Is there a chance we will run into any animals?" The thought of being attacked by a wolf was an image I was struggling to shake.

He raised his eyebrows and glanced my way. "You aren't a fan of wildlife I take it?"

"I don't dislike animals. I just don't feel like getting attacked by a bear or a wolf or something."

He flashed me that sexy grin, and my heart went into overdrive.

"You won't be attacked, and I have my permit to carry, anyway." He slid his knee to the side so I could see his gun holstered in the door.

"Well, I can tell you're a woods guy."

He laughed. "A woods guy, huh?"

"Yeah. I hope you're a better shot with a gun than you are with a bow."

He made a choking sound. "Ouch. That hurts." He punched his chest with his fist. "It was a bad day, okay? Plus, the only thing you really need to worry about is ticks."

"Hey, I've rolled my high socks over my pants. I don't wear them like this to make a fashion statement. I live in Minnesota. I'm not stupid."

He took a left and I read the sign. "Ski Trail Road, huh?"

"Yep, great for cross country skiing but also quite challenging. A lot of rolling hills."

"Well, looks like my calves and shins are going to be hating me tomorrow."

We got out of the car and walked to the start of the trail.

"This is Big Hole Trail Loop," Troy said, pointing at the sign. "Looks like it's one point eight miles. You up for that? We can always find a shorter one if that's too much for day one."

I pushed past him. "I think I'll survive."

The birds were singing in the distance. The wind was strong enough to blow my hair around and get in my mouth, but not enough to chill me.

"When we were kids, my brother Kevin and I loved to explore the woods. Our parents were doctors, and we'd spend our summers in Side Lake boating and skiing, wake boarding, biking, all that fun stuff you do when you're in the woods, as you say."

"Sounds like you guys had a lot of fun."

"When my dad would get really mean, Kevin and I would bike to the woods and we'd explore the trails. We loved to walk the trail around the lake at McCarthy's, too. We know these trails like the back of our hands. It's so peaceful out here."

His father was mean? My throat tightened at the thought. I wanted to ask what mean looked like. Was he really strict or worse? But I had no right to ask. I hardly knew him. "The woods were your escape."

"Yeah."

Troy bent over and picked up a stick that was lying on the side of the trail and inspected it closely. "A walking stick," he said, then we made our way up the trail.

"Looks more like a roasting stick to me."

He laughed. "That works, too, I guess."

"When was the last time you came out here?'

"The summer after my wife passed. I come out here when I need to think. I spent most days working in my store to get it remodeled, but sometimes I couldn't work. I feel the most at peace in the woods, but home improvements keep my mind busy when I don't want to think. And my hands." He looked at me. "How about you?"

"Me?"

"Yeah, what do you do to keep your mind busy when you're stressed out or sad?"

"I always worked. I'd work doubles or midnights, and it helped to focus on something else instead of my unhappy marriage. For years, I tried to convince myself I was happy. Ben isn't a bad guy. We just weren't right for each other."

"Usually when people get divorced, they blame each

other, and it takes a lot of time to realize they were at fault, too. It shows a lot about the kind of person you are. I respect that."

I never thought about it that way. Ben really was a good guy. My brother even liked him, and my brother never liked my boyfriends. He never liked my sister's boyfriends, either. "It's hard to say anything bad about Ben. He wasn't controlling or mean. Most of the time, we did our own thing."

Troy stopped suddenly and put his hand out to hold me back.

"Wha—"

I stared at the big black bear as he walked across the path and into the woods. I held my breath, waiting for him to see us and attack. Why wasn't Troy reaching for his gun? He just stood there with his arm out.

"Stay still," he whispered. "Don't move."

I did what he said, though every part of me wanted to scream and run in the other direction. The bear was gone, and yet I kept holding my breath, and my legs shook.

Troy lowered his arm. "Okay, he's gone."

I let out a long exhale. "Okay, he's gone? Are you kidding me? You think I'm going to keep walking in the direction he was just heading? No. No way."

I turned around and started walking back in the direction we had come.

He grabbed my hand. "Do you know the odds of him coming back here? Bears are more scared of you than you are of them. If we got in between a black bear and their cub, it would probably be a much bigger problem."

I shrugged out of his hold and kept walking back to the car at a fast speed, all the while trying to be as light on my feet as I could. My heart had not slowed down a bit. I just wanted to reach the car and have something solid in between me and Mother Nature.

Five more steps and Troy grabbed onto my shoulder and stopped me. I turned around to yell at him to let me go when I saw the white stripe. Seriously? A skunk? It ran across the path in front of us and into the woods. This hike was enough to keep me locked inside Tim's house for the summer.

Once it was far gone, Tim said, "Okay. You can keep walking."

"How are you so calm right now? We could have been sprayed!"

"But we weren't," he said. "It's all about not startling the animals. You need to let them know you're in the woods. It'll be much easier next time. The odds of seeing bears, or even skunks in the woods, are pretty slim."

"You seriously think you're getting me into the woods again? You have to be kidding me. Not happening, buddy."

He laughed and followed me the last few feet to the car.

Once safely inside, I put my hand on my heart to steady my breathing.

"You okay?"

"Am I okay? I was in the woods not even half an hour and a bear almost ate me and I was almost sprayed by a skunk. No, I'm not okay. Now, please take me back to Tim's house. I want to hide inside for the next month."

He put his hand on my thigh and patted it. It may have been a friendly gesture, but his touch made me lose my breath all over again.

Chapter 9

Lizzy

I drove up to Troy's house at dinnertime with a car full of all my stuff. Thankfully, my landlord had let me out of my rental contract two months early because he had someone interested in renting the apartment. Now I was looking forward to a weekend with our friends, boating, and just relaxing. The weather was supposed to be warm and rain was only expected on Sunday.

Although I was not happy about facing Tim again, I was grateful he promised not to ask me questions about why I said no to his proposal. I wanted to be in the same room as him without being uncomfortable. Maybe we weren't there yet, but it was my goal to get there. Two years had come and gone. I was not sure why he still cared, anyway. I would not let our strained relationship impede my summer.

I would always be attracted to Tim, but I did not want to be with him. I hardly knew him at all, and if he really wanted to be with me, he would have hunted me down. Sure, he sent a few texts, but he did not try that hard. We only dated a few months, anyway. Hopefully, he had his closure now.

"You're here just in time for dinner. Everyone is coming over to eat and sauna. Hopefully you know where your swimsuit is in all that stuff," Troy said, pointing to my suitcases.

Luckily, the apartment I lived in was fully furnished, so I did not have a lot of stuff. I was still wearing most of the clothes Victoria bought me two years ago. I needed little since all I did was work and go to school, so I lived in my scrubs.

"Of course I do. I'll put on my suit under my clothes and then I'll help you with dinner. And don't tell me you don't need my help, okay?'

Troy dropped his shoulders. "Fine. You're so bossy." He squeezed my shoulder. "It's great to have you around again."

"It's great to be back," I said. The drive to Virginia where I worked and went to school was only a forty-five minute drive. He and I both knew I could have made that drive every day if I wanted to. Instead, I moved away because I was running. Running from the pain.

I picked up a suitcase and Troy picked up the other one and we made our way to my old bedroom. My chest burned when he shut the door. I wanted to go into the kitchen and watch Victoria make dinner and cook pies. I wanted to watch Troy chase her around the house to tickle her when she tried to kick him out of the kitchen for digging into the pies before they were cool. I missed the advent calendar with doors we had to open up every day with new obstacles that ended up keeping us all together and overcoming our fears as a group. I missed my friends, and it was time to stop sulking and start living again.

. . .

I began unpacking my suitcase and froze when my hand reached the felt box. For a moment, I had forgotten I packed the box. I sat on the bed and opened it. A silver key stared back at me. I was not sure what the key was for, but I knew there had to be some reason Victoria gave it to me for Christmas. I asked her many times what it was for and she kept telling me, "You'll see." But she was gone before I found out. Right then and there, I decided my mission for the summer was to have fun, relax, and discover the secret of the key.

When I made it back into the kitchen, Troy was nowhere to be found. I peeked my head out the sliding glass door and found him on the patio, grilling burgers and chicken.

"How's it going? What can I help you with?"

"Just in time. Could you grab the baked potatoes on the counter? They're wrapped in aluminum foil. Be careful. They are still hot. Everyone will be here any minute, so I might as well put the burgers on the grill.

I grabbed a bowl and collected the plate of potatoes. A voice from behind startled me and I dropped a potato on the floor, butter and oil leaking out of the foil. "Shit!"

I turned my head to see who would do that to me, and then I laughed.

Brad was standing there staring at me and waving his hands with a baseball gesture. "Safe!"

"You jerk," I said with a laugh. Brad was always full of mischief. Sometimes he reminded me of a child. Usually the jokes weren't on me, so it made me happy to see he felt comfortable enough with me to joke around.

"I wouldn't laugh," I said. "That potato was yours."

"I don't eat carbs," he said, patting his stomach.

"I highly doubt that."

I hardly blinked before he lunged at me and held the bowl above my head. I had to jump to reach it.

"Give me those potatoes or I'm calling Maddy!"

The door slammed, and we both looked to see who had busted us.

"Brad, really?" Maddy rolled her eyes and set David down. He ran over and gave me a hug.

"You've gotten so big, buddy. How old are you now? Ten? Eleven?"

"Six," he said with a slur. His two front teeth were missing.

"Buddy, when did you lose your teeth?"

"My dad helped me wiggle them out. We tried floss and slammed a door, it was so cool."

"Daddy always has the best ideas," Maddy said with a bit of sarcasm in her tone. She looked at Brad and he smiled.

"What can I say? I'm the fun parent."

Maddy just shook her head and walked up to hug me.

"Can't take him anywhere," she said in a loud enough whisper for Brad to hear. She crouched and helped David tie his shoe. "Why don't we go outside and see what Uncle Troy is doing?"

"Can I help him flip burgers, mama? Please?"

I took the bowl from Brad's hands when he wasn't paying attention and followed Maddy and David out of the door.

"Hey, you can't do that. I wasn't looking."

"Sucks to be you," I said over my shoulder.

Ten minutes later, the patio was full our friends, plus all the laughter and loud chatter that came along with them.

I felt a tap on my shoulder and turned around to find Olivia standing behind me.

"How's it going? You aching to take some vitals or what?"

I laughed and hugged her. "I can't thank you enough for all the time you helped me study.'

"How does it feel?"

"Amazing. I can't wait to get my first job as an official R.N."

"You deserve it. I will never forget my first paycheck as a nurse. Thirty bucks an hour was my starting rate. Going from making minimum wage plus tips at a coffee shop to that was quite the shock. Sadly, you get used to it and the more money you make, the more bills you seem to have."

Kevin walked up behind us and put his hands around our shoulders. "Isn't that the truth? What would I know? I'm just a cop."

"Sheriff," Lyndsey said. "Don't let him fool you. He makes good money, but he should make more for what he does."

I nodded. "Yeah, you'd think putting your life on the line every day would be a better-paying job."

"More like constant criticism," Kevin said. "But I like what I do. I enjoy helping people."

"Don't let him fool you," Lyndsey said with a wink. "He's a badass."

We all laughed.

I looked over at Troy. He kept staring at Olivia.

Something was definitely brewing up there. Olivia was peeking at Troy, then she took water out of the cooler.

"Have you ever shot anyone?" I said to Kevin, trying to be funny.

His eyes widened, and he took a big gulp of his beer.

"Seriously?"

"Got you," he said with a laugh. "Although I did almost shoot my ex-wife this one time."

Lyndsey punched his shoulder. "Don't even joke like that. That's terrible."

"What? It's true," he said. "Okay, maybe it isn't true, but I got to watch her get tazered and that was even better."

"I can't believe I didn't get to see that," Troy said. "Now everyone, dig in before the burgers get cold."

Chapter 10

Olivia

"Where did you go today?"

"Excuse me?" How did Tim know I even left?

Tim's head disappeared into the closet and popped back out. His house was small and probably more like a cabin, but I was starting to adjust. It was comfy and felt like home.

"I noticed the tire tracks in the mud outside. I'm pretty sure you only know my friends, so I was just wondering if you did anything fun today."

He knew, but did it really matter? Nothing was going on between Troy and I other than some harmless flirting. I felt a little guilty because of my recent divorce and Troy's situation, but flirting with him was fun. I had done nothing wrong.

"Troy invited me to go hiking with him, and it was the worst experience I've ever had."

He deadpanned. "Did he make a move on you?"

I laughed. "No. I can handle myself if he tried anything, but no." I shook my head. "He took me to the trails over by Bimbos and we ran into a bear face-to-face.

"You're kidding, right?. How is this the first I am hearing of it?'

"Obviously, I survived, and it's fine, but I'm not sure I will go hiking again soon."

"Didn't he have his gun?"

"Yes, he had his gun. It's not like we were attacked."

I put on my jacket and he followed me out the door. "Did you expect him to shoot the bear for crossing paths with us?"

"I just worry about the baby."

"Hey, what about me?"

He laughed. "Well, you matter, too. Kinda."

I kicked rocks at him.

The wind was refreshing as it made its way around the pine trees and blew my hair enough to bother me. I grabbed my hair in my hand and twisted it over my shoulder. My dark curls were always frizzy unless I spent time applying gel and shaking it up. I spent so many hours on my hair so Ben would look at me, but here I felt free. Like how I looked didn't matter. My new friends weren't as high maintenance as my friends back in the cities. When I worked at the hospital, we were all too exhausted to care. But if we went out after work, we had to look perfect. How exhausting.

We made our way up Troy's driveway.

"Well...have you told Troy about..." He looked down at my stomach.

"No, I haven't told him, and I don't want to tell anyone right now."

I put my hand on my still flat stomach.. I felt a little swelling when I touched it, but not enough for anyone to notice. "I'll say something when I'm ready. Right now, I'm not ready for all the questions."

"They aren't like that. My friends aren't judgmental.

They like to joke around, but they are supportive and friendly. They're the kind of people who would give you the shirt off their backs."

"Or take me in for the summer," I said with a closed lip smile.

"That's right," he said. "Now you can't say I've never done anything for you."

We stopped a few feet before Troy's door.

"Are you sure going back to work is a good idea? That wasn't what I meant by relaxing this summer."

"I really wanted to relax and I still plan on it, but I think it will be good for me to have a reason to get up early and I've never not worked. I'm just there per diem, so I'll be picking up shifts. I told HR I'm pregnant, and they want to work with me, but I don't want the supervisor or staff to know yet."

"I'm happy for you, but I don't mind helping you out financially if you decide not to work."

I leaned in and hugged him. "Thank you for taking care of me, little brother. I'll be just fine, okay? Stop worrying."

I opened the door and stepped in behind him. Troy's house was elegant and had a nice lake vibe to it. I could tell immediately that Victoria had decorated the house. I loved the giant floor to ceiling windows and the blue and pink floral design throughout the kitchen. The high ceiling and visible loft with the log staircase gave it that natural woodsy atmosphere. My dream house.

"I love the ceilings and everything about this place," I whispered.

"Just wait until you see the movie theater in the basement," Tim said. "Me and the boys worked for months on it. It's unbelievable. Wait until you see it."

I was never really much of a TV or movie person. I

would sit on the couch and read a book while everyone else was glued to the television. Ben always said I was being rude, but I never understood what was so rude about sitting in the room staring at a television or reading a book. He said it was weird when I didn't laugh with him and he didn't have anyone to make comments to, but I always listened when he talked about the show he was watching. Video entertainment just wasn't my thing. A reminder of why it would never work out between the two of us.

Everyone welcomed us into the backyard. They were genuinely happy to see us. My social anxiety disappeared once again. Normally, I'd make up some excuse not to attend social gatherings. I would stay home and read a book or put in a yoga workout video. I never had friends I couldn't wait to be around. But these people wanted me to join them, and I was grateful.

"Can I get you a drink?" Maddy asked.

"I've got it, Maddy," Troy said. "All the food is inside. Help yourself. Let me get you guys something to drink."

"I'll get you a plate," Tim said. "Have a seat and relax."

Was he upset I'd spent the day with Troy, or was he just worried about me being pregnant and wanted to pamper me? I decided he was probably just trying to be helpful. My brother was anything but controlling.

Tim came back with a plate of food for both of us, and Kat followed behind with Tim's guitar.

"Look what I found," she said, holding the guitar out to him. "You left it at Kevin's house from the last bonfire. We can't have a bonfire without entertainment."

Tim shook his head. Although he acted confident and his voice gave everyone goosebumps, he was humble. He had no idea how good he was. He always blinked at the ladies while he sang. My friends said he would smile at a woman as if she was the only person in the room and like he'd written the song just for her. But I knew the genuine person behind that facade. He was broken inside, and he fooled everyone, including himself.

"I think you should sing with me tonight, Liv," he said.

I looked down at my plate to hide my face. Heat crept up my neck and warmed my cheeks. Although my skin was tan, my dad being half Italian and all, I still felt like everyone could see through my nerves.

"Don't pull me into this," I said.

"You sing?" Kat said.

"Please sing for us tonight," Maddy said.

Tim grinned. "We're going to bug you until you say yes. Trust me, this group is relentless."

"Whose side are you on, anyway?"

He stuck out his tongue, and everyone laughed.

"Fine," I said.

I was not one to bring attention to myself if I didn't have to, but Tim always talked me into it. He did not understand what it was like to be sensitive and shy. I struggled with it my whole life, but the rest of my family was so outgoing. Despite my shyness, we sang very well together. Our voices complimented each other. We even sang together at weddings and a few funerals, and open mic night in the Cities.

As the sun went down, everyone gathered around the fire.

Tim tuned his guitar, and he strummed the first note of *Shallow*, one of my all-time favorite songs. I stood up to sing because I needed a lot of power to hit a note with as much passion as Lady Gaga.

My stomach twisted in knots, and I took deep, steady breaths to prepare myself. I closed my eyes, afraid to see the looks on their faces if I was out of tune. The world around me vanished as I felt every note deep in my soul. I was no longer in control of my body or my emotions.

I opened my eyes and looked at my brother as we hit the chorus together. I smiled, and he grinned back. I had forgotten about the high I got when I sang. I suddenly had superpowers, and I stopped thinking about the words and continued to feel them. My self- sabotaging behavior disappeared, and my emotions ran deep.

The song ended and everyone was silent. I was panting and my brain slipped into an overly critical self-destruction mode. Did I sound okay? Did I sing too loud? Did I embarrass myself?

I sat down on the chair and pursed my lips together. Everyone was just staring at us, mainly me.

Maddy stood up and started clapping, then Kat, Lyndsey, Brad, everyone. My eyes landed on Troy, and he stared at me in disbelief. Their clapping continued to get louder, but I wasn't good at taking compliments or praise and I felt my face burning up. I sat on my hands and looked away.

When Tim brushed away my tears with his sleeve, I realized I was crying.

I laughed. I felt this year crashing down on me. The divorce, the baby, my brother's kindness. I thought I lost everything, but now my life was all coming together. I was surrounded by new friends.

"Your brother blew us away when he sang for us the first time, but wow, your voice, it's just so…" Ethan stopped to think.

"Beautiful," Maddy said.

"Perfect," Kat said.

Lyndsay held up her arms. "I got chills."

"You guys are too kind, but thank you."

"My sister struggles with compliments. She always has," Tim said.

I looked over to Troy, but his chair was empty. He had disappeared into the darkness. Did he hate the song? The spiral of self-doubt circled in my head.

Chapter 11

Lizzy

"You blew us all away tonight with your voice, Olivia. God, it was beautiful," I said. "It was so emotional Troy had to walk away to wipe his tears." I wanted to see if Liv reacted to my words, but I had a hard time reading her. She looked deep in thought.

"Thank you, but it's my brother that's the entertainer. I'd never do that alone."

How could she not sing every chance she had to show off a voice like that? "Give yourself more credit, Liv. You were phenomenal." I put a hand over my heart and swooned at the memory of how her voice made me feel. " I could feel every word, every emotion. Ugh."

She waved me off. It was obvious she struggled with compliments.

We were the first ones in the sauna. Everyone else was changing or helping Troy clean up. Tim came in next and sat down next to Olivia. He was avoiding me.

"Lizzy's right, sis, you should sing more."

"Stop," she said, brushing him off. "Is there a wet towel

around? I'm having a hard time breathing in here. I need to put it over my face."

Tim jumped up. "Oh crap, I don't think pregnant women are supposed to be in a sauna."

My eyes widened. I looked at Olivia, then at her stomach. Was she pregnant?

"Really, Tim? I asked you not to say anything and here you are blabbing. I can't trust you to keep just one secret for me."

She stormed out of the sauna and slammed the sauna door.

Tim went after her, but I stepped in front of him. He tried to walk past me, but I put my arm out. "Give her a minute, trust me."

He gave me a confused look, and then his shoulders slumped. "She's going to kill me. I promised I wouldn't say anything. She didn't want anyone to find out yet."

"I can't believe she's pregnant. Is this a good thing?"

He covered his eyes with his hand. "She says it is. I'm such an idiot."

"You did the right thing. Saunas aren't recommended during pregnancy, especially the first trimester. Looking at her, she can't be very far along. She doesn't even have a baby bump yet."

He sat in front of me on the bench and I put my hands on his shoulders. He rested his head back on my lap and I started running my fingers through his hair.

This was a bad idea.

"I'm surprised she didn't realize that," he said. "She's a nurse."

"She probably just forgot. She's not used to being pregnant. She's probably more caught off guard because she didn't think about it than the fact that you told me. She can't do hot tubs either. The warm temperature can harm the baby and increase the risk of birth defects."

"You're right. I'm glad I said something, but I should have been more discreet." He lifted his head off me. "Sorry, I didn't mean to—"

I didn't mean to either, but it felt so good to touch him again, even if it was just to support and calm him.

We both sat there in silence until Kevin and Ethan walked in and sat down.

"Is your sister okay? She ran across the road pretty fast. I think she was going home, maybe. She looked mad," Brad said.

"Yeah, I should go check on her." Tim got to his feet. He put his hand on the door and then turned back to look at me with a friendly smile.

I smiled back, and then he was gone.

After a few drinks and the warm sauna, everyone was calling it a night an hour later.

"We just have one dock to put in tomorrow and then we'll take the boat out," Kevin said.

"Kevin's right." Ethan said.

Kevin looked at Ethan. "Yep. Let's start early so we can get out on the lake by noon. How does eight sound?"

"Works for me. How about you ladies?" Ethan said. "Any of you want to help with the dock?"

"If you need me, I'm there, but I was thinking us girls could get together and make food for boating and for dinner. What do you guys think?"

"Sounds like a lot more fun than putting the boat in," I said.

"Let's head over to Kat's. She has the biggest kitchen," Maddy said.

Kat nodded. "Works for me. The B&B is booked with a sizeable group of friends who are planning on going four wheeling up north in Bear River. They'll be gone pretty early."

I helped grab some towels from the change room in the sauna and followed Troy into the house as everyone left.

Troy raised his eyebrows. "Well, did you have a good time?"

"I did. It was the best night I've had in a long time. I laughed a lot, and I really like Liv. She's a great addition."

"Mmm hmm," Troy mumbled under his breath.

He was definitely thinking about Olivia, but he would never admit it, so I avoided it instead.

His eyes had dark circles under them. "Are you tired?"

I yawned on cue. "I'm pretty tired."

He raised an eyebrow. "Too tired to watch a movie in the basement?"

I perked up. "Absolutely not. As long as I get to pick the movie."

"Deal," he said. "Which movie?"

"Fargo," I said with a laugh.

"Yah, you betcha. I'll grab the water and meet you in the basement in five."

"Hey, Troy."

He turned back. "Yeah."

"I want to show you something."

He followed me to my bedroom, and I pulled out the key. "Victoria gave me this for Christmas before she passed, but she never told me what it was for. Do you know?"

He took the key from me and examined it closely. "I

think it's a safe deposit box or a PO Box key. I can't believe she gave you a key and didn't even tell you about it."

"Right? At the time, I didn't think about it. I figured she'd tell me when she was ready," I said.

"Makes sense, but I know my wife and if she didn't tell you, it was for a reason."

"Do you think we should try to figure it out?'

Troy nodded. "Why don't we try on Tuesday, after the holiday weekend is over and everything is open again? I'd think it would have to be Hibbing or even the post office here in Side Lake."

"I'd love to, but how about Wednesday instead? I have to work on Tuesday."

"I could close up the shop early on Wednesday. Not a problem."

"Or you could ask Olivia to pick up a couple of hours."

He looked like he was thinking about it. "Do you think she would? What about her job?"

"She works on Tuesday with me and we are both off Wednesday."

He fidgeted. "Maybe. I have a retired teacher that loves to help out and Emma said she wants to help out, too. I'm not sure it's something Olivia wants to do."

"How do you know if you don't ask her?"

"Yeah, I guess," he said with a shrug. "I just don't really know her that well yet. I don't want her to feel like she has to."

"I think she'd love to," I said. I had a feeling she wouldn't mind being closer to Troy. Maybe he felt the same.

Chapter 12

Olivia

I woke up with my face on a wet pillow and my body in the fetal position.

After I got back from Troy's, I locked myself in my room so Tim could not follow me. I was surprised when he didn't arrive until thirty minutes after I got home. Did Lizzy stop him to give me a head start? Would Lizzy tell everyone I was pregnant? I had a feeling she was not the kind of person to gossip. I had to trust her, and I did. More than I trusted my brother, anyway. He couldn't keep his big mouth shut.

I heard a light tapping on my door. I had no choice but to respond. He knew I was in here.

"Come in," I said.

My back was to the door. I did not realize he was by my bed until I felt his weight on the mattress shift my body. I rolled over, but I waited to hear him speak.

"I'm so sorry I blurted out your secret."

I glared at him. No way was I letting him off that easily.

"I was worried about the baby, and I blurted it out

without thinking. But you don't need to worry about Lizzy. She won't tell anyone."

I sat up and he shifted his weight back.

"That's not the point, Tim. She's going to worry about me, just like you now. I'm annoyed that I can't trust you with a secret. It wasn't your secret to tell."

I was being a little unreasonable, but I was angry. He did not think or give me the chance to tell her my secret. Lizzy and I had gotten so close. What if she felt betrayed? Would she be on me all the time about doing anything that might affect the baby? No, she wasn't like that.

My eyes teared up.

"I know it wasn't my secret to tell, but you can trust her. It's nice you have a female you can talk to now. I know the two of you have gotten close."

"I'm hormonal and emotional, and I'm not ready to forgive you right now. I think I could consider it though, if you tell me what happened with you and Lizzy."

He tried to stand up, but I grabbed his arm and pulled him back down.

"I don't want to talk about it," he said through clenched teeth.

"Yes, you do. You love her."

He turned his head away.

"You do!" I knew he did.

He jerked his head my way and got to his feet. "It doesn't matter. She doesn't want to be with me."

"How do you know?"

His hands were in fists, and his face was red with rage mixed with a bit of sadness.

"I asked her to marry me and do you know what she said? She said no and then she ran away. Now here we are two years later." He looked defeated.

I shook my head, not believing my ears. "Wait a minute. You asked her to marry you? When?"

"A couple of years ago. I tried texting her many times, but she wouldn't talk to me."

"A couple of years ago? Tim, she was probably grieving. Was it right after Victoria died?"

He said nothing.

"Tim, you need to tell her you still feel that way. You're a catch. She'd be stupid to keep running."

"I tried. She didn't want me. I even took her out in the canoe so she couldn't run, but she still did." He hid his face in his hands.

"You need to keep trying. I see the way she looks at you. Don't give up on her."

He took two steps toward the door. "I don't think my heart can take it, Liv. I just don't think I can. It broke me."

I knew when not to keep pushing, so instead I said, "By the way, you're forgiven in case you're wondering. Just sew that mouth shut, okay?"

He peeked his head back in the door. "Deal."

We all stood around Kat's tall table, making sandwiches and packing a cooler.

"It's going to be close to seventy degrees today," Kat said.

Maddy nodded. "No wind, so it won't be extremely cold on the boat."

Lyndsey took the cap off the Mayo. "If that's the case, I'm skiing."

I stopped spreading the bread and gasped. "You're kidding, right? Isn't the water freezing?"

Kat laughed. "Lyndsey is our dye hard skier, Liv. She doesn't care."

"I wait all year for this. A little ice cold water doesn't hurt you as long as you don't fall in."

I just shook my head. "You're brave." I leaned in toward her. "Are you really going to ski?"

"You bet I am. We only have a few good months of summer, and I'm not wasting one day where I could be in the water."

"Liv, do you ski?" Maddy asked.

"I grew up on Lake Superior, so we went boating a lot, but we did a little skiing. Now that lake is cold. I went a couple times to other lakes with my friends, but I was never great at it."

Lyndsey squeezed my arm. "Are you going to try? I could teach you?"

I caught Lizzy's gaze. "No, not today. I'm much better at cheering."

"I like that," Lyndsey said. "I need someone I trust to pay attention, so when I fall, the boat stops. Last year, we had a few issues." Lyndsey glared at Kat.

"I'm sorry, okay? Ethan kept distracting me with cat fail videos. It was one time."

"Twice," Lyndsey said.

"Okay, twice. But I haven't done it since."

"That was our last time skiing last summer. You have yet to redeem yourself." She leaned into my ear and whispered, "Don't trust her. She has no attention span and gets easily distracted by the famous author of Side Lake."

I was confused. Was this a joke? "Famous author?"

Lizzy tossed the chips in the basket on top of the last sandwich. "Have you ever heard of Elizabeth Conrad?"

I tried to read her. Was this a joke? "Elizabeth Conrad

is one of my favorite authors of all time. Are you kidding me? Who doesn't know who Elizabeth Conrad is?"

Maddy snorted. "You've met her."

I shook my head. "What? No, I haven't. Do you know her?"

Kat cleared her throat. "Elizabeth Conrad is Ethan's pen name."

My forehead scrunched up. I looked around at all of them. "Is this another joke?"

"Nope. You would never know, right? He's so humble. He doesn't talk about it. That's why we are doing the float and try to center it around his books. Isn't that awesome?"

Lyndsey was serious. Ethan really was Elizabeth Conrad.

"When you guys said Ethan was a famous writer the other day I had no idea he was her. Or she was him. This is unbelievable!"

Kat flipped her hair behind her shoulder. "Yeah, I married her. Jealous?"

"I'm sorry, I'm just in shock. That's unbelievable. I've read every one of her—his books. I can't believe my brother never told me."

"He isn't really one to talk about his personal life, is he?" Lizzy said when everyone took off to fill the cooler with water and pop and to get towels for the boat.

"He's always struggled with opening up. Is that why the two of you broke up?"

Great way to be subtle. I hoped she hadn't caught how awkward that transition was.

"Partly. I like you Liv, so I don't want to put you in the middle, but he and I just didn't work out."

"Is it because of the way he acts? He can seem cocky at

times, but he's actually really humble. Girls always seem to get scared off by his confidence."

"It isn't that. It was just getting a bit...serious, and I wasn't ready. I needed space, and he never came after me. Maybe that sounds stupid," she said.

I put my hand on her shoulder. "That's not stupid at all. You were going through a lot. Do you miss him?"

She looked away. Obviously, she did.

"It would never work out between us. We had our chance."

"Never say never," I said. "My brother is smitten with you. Don't give up on him, okay?"

She smiled. "Let's not talk about this anymore. How about we carry some of these bags to the dock, okay?"

I was so close to finding answers, but she was not ready to share. My brother would have to fight harder. These two were meant to be. I could feel it in my bones.

Chapter 13

Lizzy

The boys picked us up around noon, as expected. Ethan stayed behind with Kat because they had an issue with their air conditioner.

"Go, we'll catch up later," Ethan said.

We were picking up Maddy after David's nap. Tim, Liv, Troy, Lyndsey, Brad, and Kevin were on the boat, and that meant there was no escaping Tim. Kevin drove the boat while Troy and Olivia ended up in the front of the boat. Tim, Lyndsey, Brad, and I sat in the back.

Lyndsey put on her life jacket, and Kevin turned off the boat in the middle of the lake to dig out the rope. Lyndsey jumped in the water and I got splashed. The freezing water took my breath away, yet she was not complaining, even though half her body was in the freezing cold water.

"How do you not have hypothermia? That water is ice cold." I leaned over the side of the boat and stuck my hand in. "Maybe it's not as bad as I thought."

"That's because you're only feeling the top of the water. Reach in a little farther," Troy said.

I did as he said and just a few inches down, the water was so cold my hand went numb. "Yep, that's cold."

"Ready?" Kevin said to Lyndsey.

"Ready!"

The engine revved, and she was immediately pulled to her feet. She was all over the place, dropping a ski, then going barefoot. She put the rope behind her back and turned around in a full circle. She was unbelievable. Aunt Victoria and Uncle Troy had told me she was a good skier, but I never imagines she would be this good.

At one point, I was completely turned around watching her, and Tim's leg bumped into mine when wc went over a giant wave. I looked into his eyes and then turned away as quick as it happened.

Staying away from him was going to be harder than I thought.

Brad was the only other person who was crazy enough to get into the water. Not a big surprise since they were siblings. Brad was as good on a wake boarder as Lyndsey was on skis. I kept my eyes on them for fear of missing one of their tricks. They were flawless and their posture and poise showed their expertise and made it look so easy.

The jumps were unbelievable to watch, but once Kevin started doing flips, that's when my mouth fell open. I squealed when he landed each one of his flips as if they were a simple feat. He was a gymnast, an acrobat.

Five minutes later, he dropped the rope and announced he was getting back in the boat. As we circled him, I noticed his lips were turning blue.

"Cold, brother?" Lyndsey said.

"I won't lie. When that sun goes behind the clouds it's freezing out here."

"And when you drop into the water," Lyndsey said. She

reached over the side of the boat to grab the wakeboard from him.

We drove around the lake for the next hour, picking up Maddy, David, and Ethan from the shore. I moved up to the front and sat next to Liv, glad I did not have to sit directly next to Tim.

"Beautiful day, but cold," Olivia said.

We both had on sweatshirts and towels tucked beneath our legs.

"Freezing," I said. My hands were numb from the cold air.

Troy took over driving the boat, and we made our way around Big Sturgeon, the largest lake on the chain. The wind was stronger on this lake, but surprisingly, it did not bother me. Our bodies bounced with the rough waves, and my dark curls were whipping all over the place. Multiple times, I had to pull my hair out of my mouth, but the boat ride was so much fun I did not want it to end. A few other boats were in the water, but none of the boaters swam. We did see little kids jumping into the shallow, warmer water.

Swans and loons swam or flew away as our boat approached. At one point, I covered my eyes because I was sure Troy would run over two loons in our path. When I opened my eyes, they had both disappeared beneath the waves and I let out the air I'd been holding in. They were much quicker than I thought.

Troy cut the engine once we slipped under the bridge to our lake on West Sturgeon.

Liv and I both looked back at Troy, waiting for an explanation.

He stood up and peeled off his shirt. "Anyone else want to jump in with me?"

"Why not," I said.

I didn't stop to peel off my shirt before I dove into the water from the front of the boat. Kevin ran and jumped off the boat right after me, doing a cannon ball way too close to me. I dipped under so I would not choke on the water from his giant splash.

I glanced back at Liv to see if she would jump in. She was standing on the back plank next to Troy. They were chatting and holding hands.

"Liv! Come on!"

"I can't. I changed my mind. It's too cold!"

She was on one foot, her other foot dipping into the lake while she held onto Troy's hand to find her balance. Brad made his way to the back of the boat and pushed Troy in, accidentally taking Olivia with him.

I swam around to the back of the boat to make sure she was okay.

She was gasping and crying out. "It's so cold! You jerk," she said, laughing and coughing at the same time.

"Oops, sorry about that," Brad said, with little sympathy in his tone.

She splashed him, and he leaned back, avoiding the water. He did a giant cannon ball next to them, and they both cried out. Troy helped Olivia back into the boat and then dunked Brad under the water.

Brad came out of the water laughing and splashed Troy before climbing into the boat. His muscles bulged as he pulled himself in. "In you go, Lizzy." He reached for my hand, and in one swift motion, I was on my feet and now in the back of the boat.

The cold water dripped all over the seat as I searched for a towel, my body shaking.

Tim wrapped his huge towel around my body. I was so cold I could neither speak nor resist the warmth of his small touch. I wanted to think I could do this without his help, but at the same time, I could not resist. My teeth chattered, so he pulled me onto the seat next to him and rubbed my arms over the blanket. I tucked my face into his warm sweatshirt.

"Okay, everybody, it's time to make our way to shore before the sun sets."

I felt warm as long as I was touching Tim. His body heat radiated off his tight core and soft hands. I would over-think this later, but for now, it felt so good. I wanted it. I was sick of fighting the chemistry between us.

Chapter 14

Olivia

I never would have jumped into that lake if it wasn't for Brad pushing Troy and taking me along. The water was colder than I ever expected, but it was also thrilling. I stepped out of my normal comfort zone. I always liked to take the safe route and try to blend in. I liked to be comfortable in a safe place. Risks just led to anxiety and who wanted anxiety in their life?

I was surprised to find that my body could warm up, and I would not die of hypothermia. I could not stop smiling at the thrill of doing something risky. I feared so many things and I had so many questions.

Would I be a good mom?

Who cared? Who really cared? If I knew what every person was thinking about my choices, I'd do nothing. I was sick of hiding. Did I really know who I was or was I just trying to impress everyone around me? Was this the role model I wanted to be for my child?

Life is messy. It's really messy and my mission for this summer was finding out who I was, not the person everyone expected me to be. Now that I had supportive friends who were open to letting me be who I was, this was the perfect time to find myself.

The rain poured all day Sunday and Monday. We spent the rest of the weekend playing cards and watching movies in Troy's movie theater. By Tuesday, I was regretting my choice to go back to work. I was only eleven weeks pregnant, but I felt exhausted and nauseous all the time. I wasn't throwing up, but some days getting out of bed took everything in me.

Lizzy picked me up at five thirty in the morning, before the sun was awake.

She did a double take when I got into the car. "Are you okay? You look a little green."

"Yeah, just a little sick to my stomach this morning."

"You sure you're going to be okay?"

"Yeah, I'm fine." I pulled saltines out of my bag. "As long as there aren't any strong smells and I don't let my stomach get empty, I'll be fine."

"Okay. If you're sure." She patted my leg. "You're tough. I admire that about you."

We put away our things in the locker room and clocked in, but we were still ten minutes early.

"Ready?" Lizzy said, taking my arm.

Was she holding my arm to steady me on my feet or was she just being friendly? Hopefully, I did not look that under the weather or everyone would start asking questions. The person in HR knew I was pregnant because I'd be taking a leave of absence once I got closer to my due date. She assured me no one else would know until I was ready to share my news.

Lizzy showed me around the maternity floor and the

nurses were all friendly. The hospital was not as nice as the one I worked at in the Cities, but it was clean and well sanitized.

A handsome man who made his scrubs look more like a Calvin Klein ad caught my attention as he snuck past me and put his arm around Lizzy.

"Here, I thought you ran away or something. Where have you been? This place falls apart without you."

"Hi, Adam," she said, brushing him off. "I want you to meet our newest RN, Olivia. Liv, meet Adam."

He held out his hand, but his eyes were still on Lizzy. What was the story between them, because they obviously had a connection? The chemistry was undeniable. Lizzy was avoiding eye contact with him, but not because she didn't want to look at him. She was bashful and totally into him.

Poor Tim.

My brother had better step up his game, or this prince would swoop in on his girl. And I would not get in the way of the heat. Of course, I loved my brother, but I wanted Lizzy to be happy and if my brother was dumb enough to let her go without a fight, that was on him.

"Adam is our supervisor."

Oh no. The supervisor had a crush on her? No wonder she would not look at him.

"Why don't you show her around the unit, Lizzy?" He looked at me. "Did Lizzy tell you she's transitioning into an RN in the next week or two?"

She did not. "Congratulations, Lizzy. I can't believe you forgot to mention that to me." I bumped her with my hip.

"You guys must be close." Adam said. "You never told me about Liv. How do the two of you know each other?"

"We're neighbors," Lizzy said.

A guilty look crossed Lizzy's face. She was avoiding telling him I was her ex-boyfriend's sister. I held my fist in front of my face to keep from laughing. She was totally into him. Good for her.

By lunchtime, my feet were killing me, but Lizzy insisted we walk across the street to the park and have our lunch. She carried a cooler and led the way around the wall that surrounded the park.

Olcott Park was huge, and a path zigzagged through the park and the two playgrounds. We made our way to another wall, and I peered over the side of the brick wall at a small pond and a water fountain.

"That is so beautiful," I said.

"Isn't it? You should see it at night when the fountain glows with beautiful lights. I love walking in the park on my break when I work midnights."

"Not by yourself, I hope. Unless it's really that safe here?"

"It can be shady at night, so I never walk the path without someone. All the nurses are usually game to walk. The path is two miles around. The Mesabi Trail is also close and goes all the way from Grand Rapids to Ely, or it will when it's finished. We should bike it one of these days and camp along the way. It would be so much fun."

Lizzy sounded so excited. I hated to crush her dreams. "I don't think I want to go into the woods for a while, not after Troy and my run-in with a bear. That was enough to traumatize me for a while."

"Eh, it's just a black bear. They only come after you if you have food or if you get in between them and their cubs. But I get it, you're pregnant, so I don't think one hundred and some miles of biking would be good for you."

"Yeah, probably not. Maybe next summer. I could have

one of those cute little baby seats on the back of my bike. Wouldn't that be fun?"

"Start 'em young," Lizzy said, handing me a sandwich.

"I can't believe you had time to make us lunches this morning. I had a hard time just finding enough energy to get out of bed."

"I'm not carrying another person in my belly." She handed me a water bottle. "And I made them last night because I knew it'd be tough getting out of bed after this weekend. I probably drank too much," Lizzy said.

"Can I ask you a question?"

She took a bite of her sandwich. "Always."

"Is there something going on between you and our sexy supervisor?"

"Adam?" she said, with a look of confusion. "No way. Why do you say that?"

"I don't know. Maybe because he's been flirting with you all day and when he talks, he is always looking your way."

She shook her head. "No, he isn't."

"Okay."

She looked at me again. "What? He doesn't."

I leaned in and nudged Lizzy. "Just so you know, I wouldn't' be upset just because you used to date my brother. I think he's cute. And if my brother let you go, then he doesn't deserve you."

"Thank you, but even if Adam has a crush on me, I'm not interested, Liv. He doesn't have a thing for me though, he's just a social guy. He makes me laugh."

"I bet he does."

Lizzy reached into the cooler and opened up a container of grapes. We munched on the grapes while we gazed at the beauty of the park. Pretty pink daisies grew in the grass in front of us. "This is the perfect place to hold events. This park is so big and beautiful. Is anything held here?"

"I believe they have concerts, and I know they hold community events here. The Land of the Loon is the big one. It's coming up in June. There are crafters and food trucks, events for kids, and music. I went last year and had a great time. All the towns up north have festivals. They take their summers seriously here."

I laughed. "Yeah, Duluth and the Cities have events like that. I've always wanted to run Grandma's Marathon, but I was never really much of a runner. It's more of a dream than a reality."

Lizzy's eyes widened. "What? Why not? You should definitely do it next year. You will be dying to get out of the house after your baby is born. Talk to Brad and Maddy, or even Kat. They're the runners, although I'm pretty sure Maddy has switched to triathlons."

I smiled. "Tim is a swimmer, too. I think they did a triathlon together a few years ago."

Maybe Lizzy did not know Tim and Maddy had a brief fling. I should really stop talking or I would get myself in trouble.

"I know they were kind of seeing each other a few years ago, but I didn't know they did a triathlon together," Lizzy said.

"He helped train her for the swimming portion, anyway. That guy is definitely a swimmer. He swims across the lake in the summer. He tried to swim the shoreline in front of our house on Lake Superior once when we were kids and I thought my mom was going to have a heart attack. She was so mad at him."

Lizzy looked at me, confused. "Because it's so cold?"

I nodded. "And because of the waves and big rocks in the water and huge boats that wouldn't be able to see him. He has no fear." Except when it came to women. Tim was scared to trust them. He always came in, expecting them to leave. Maybe because they always did, eventually.

Chapter 15

Lizzy

The rest of the day went by pretty fast. Olivia fit in with the other nurses. Her normally shy demeanor was so outgoing and confident with patients. She was a natural born leader and all the nurses quickly followed her lead despite it being her first day.

We had one newborn and four mothers in labor during our shift. It kept us all on our toes. We went from quiet to chaos in minutes and had to keep calm. I loved this part about my job, including learning how to stay calm when my heart was in overdrive. The only way to keep patients and their husbands calm was to stay calm myself. Easier said than done.

Olivia went above and beyond for each patient to make them feel comfortable. She made it look so easy. She listened to what they had to say with such kindness and an open mind. She ran, never walked, and found her way around the place rather quickly. She was a great addition to our OB unit and I couldn't have been prouder.

Dr. Evans arrived to check in on one of his high-risk patients. Shewas experiencing some complications an hour before our shift ended. Unfortunately, this doctor was not considered a great doctor nor a nice person. He did not have a good bedside manner. In my experience, he never was very good with the patients and was even worse with the nurses. He had a short fuse and was well known for being a gigantic jerk. He thought he was above us, and he lacked respect for us

"How is the mother doing in room two?" he said to no one in particular. That was another thing about him. He never looked us in the eye when he spoke. Again, no respect.

"She is in active labor and dilated to eight centimeters. Her contractions are regular and are approximately three minutes apart," Olivia said, leading the way to the mother's room.

"Okay, I can take it from here," he said, pulling back on her elbow.

She glared at him and looked at his hand on her elbow and then to me as if she could not believe what he had just done.

She shook his hand off her arm, and her teeth clenched. "Excuse me? Please don't touch me, Doctor."

He gave her a challenging look. "What is your name, nurse?"

"Olivia," she said boldly.

She was not afraid of him.

"Nurse," he said in a degrading tone. "Please get out of my way and let me do my job. Don't you have some vitals to take? You're dismissed, and I don't want to see you in here again."

Her eyes widened, and she let him pass. I squeezed her arm gently.

"Come on, let's go chart," I said.

"Does he always act like this?"

I nodded. "Unfortunately, yes. Adam has had many meetings with the board regarding his behavior, but it doesn't seem to do any good. He was just sued not too long ago for dismissing a child who needed his medical attention, and he blew off the mother multiple times, which ended in the child's appendix rupturing. He should have lost his license, but somehow the rules don't seem to apply to him. He also likes to throw random things at the nurses, like his stethoscope or his clipboard. One time he was empty-handed and took the glasses right off his face and threw them at a nurse." I shook my head at the memory.

"That's just unacceptable. I hate doctors like that," Olivia said. "And administration for not doing anything about it. They can be jerks, but usually it's because they have their patients' best interest at heart, and they fight for them. I've put up with a lot of terrible behavior from doctors, especially hot-headed ones or doctors who have no bedside manner, but I've never met a doctor that bad. Wow! It's obvious he's ready to retire."

"I know," I said. I knew I needed to try to calm Olivia. She was so upset. "I think a stop at the Sugar Shack on the way home is well deserved, don't you? They have the best bakery. You've got to try their lemon bars." I put my fingers to my lips. "They're perfection. They will take all your worries away."

Olivia took a deep breath. "That sounds like a great plan. A little sugar is a substantial reward for the long day. This baby is starving," she said, patting her belly.

We were both exhausted and hardly spoke the forty-five minutes it took us to drive home. Maddy sent a text about everyone coming over for a fish fry, but I was not feeling it. I was emotionally and physically drained and high on sugar from the bakery we devoured.

When we turned onto Greenrock Road, Olivia mentioned the situation today. "Are you okay?"

I glanced at her. "What do you mean?"

"What you witnessed today with that doctor, it must have been hard for you."

"Me? I feel terrible about what he did to you, Olivia. I've seen him do that to so many nurses and sadly, that's why they have such a high turnover rate. No one wants to be treated like that."

Olivia nodded, her eyes still on the road. "That's a shame. Some doctors understand what we do and they know we're the ones who take care of the patient, but others act like we are nobodies, not important enough to be treated with respect."

"I've seen it both ways, too. It's sad. It takes all of us to make sure our patients are well cared for. Even nurses can be that way. A couple of nurses treated me pretty terribly when I was a CNA. I learned to blow it off. Their own insecurities and past experiences made them act that way."

Olivia put her hand on mine. "You're a good person and you don't deserve that. No one does, but you're right. When they're jerks, they have pretty dark pasts or issues at home. Especially doctors and even nurses who work all the time. It isn't easy on their families," she said.

"Speaking of families, Maddy invited us to her house for fish fry."

Olivia shook her head. "I think I'll pass. I'm so exhausted. I'm going back to my brother's to crash."

"Me too," I said.

She raised her eyebrows at me.

I laughed. "I mean, I'm going back to Troy's house to crash. Not your brothers." I could feel my face heat up.

"Mmm hmm," she said, raising her eyebrows. "I really think the two of you could have been great together. It's too bad it didn't work out."

I clenched my teeth.

"I meant what I said. He may be my brother, but I'm rooting for your happiness. Whether it's with Super Adam or someone else."

My head snapped her way. "Super Adam?"

"Yeah. I think it's a cute nickname. Don't you?"

I just shook my head. "I think if you said that to his face, his head would explode. He'd probably think you were calling him a superhero. We'd never hear the end of it."

"What's wrong with that? He'd be a hot batman."

I could picture him in the dark disguise and cape. "He really would."

I lay in bed, unable to fall asleep because I could not get Adam off my mind. Did he really have a crush on me? Why did I care? He was my boss, so nothing could happen, anyway. Why did Tim keep poking his stupid, handsome face into my mind whenever I imagined Adam and me together?

I was going crazy from exhaustion. I closed my eyes and even in my dreams, I could not escape my confusing thoughts.

Chapter 16

Olivia

Tim was nowhere to be found when I arrived home. I assumed he was down at the fish fry. I was an introvert and although I loved being around people, I got most of my energy from being alone. I was great at my job and taking care of patients was what I loved to do more than anything, but it emotionally exhausted me. The stress and adrenaline rushes to the emotional journey of watching a baby be born was the most wonderful thing in the world but also left me weak and exhausted. I needed silence to get my vibe back.

When I lived with my parents, I always walked down to the lake and stared out at Lake Superior to find my peace. I loved nature, and I loved the lake. So I made my way down to the dock in front of Tim's house and gazed at the calmness before me. I took off my shoes and dipped my feet into the water.

The calm lake was clear and although I could not see the bottom, I could see fish swimming beneath my feet. The fish swam away when I kicked my feet. I never fished while growing up, it sounded so boring. I'd rather chill out at home reading a book in my favorite reading spot in a hammock tied between two trees at the back of my parents' house. Now I could hardly wait until summer when I would float around the lake on an inflatable bed. I assumed it would have to be during the week, since weekends were probably pretty busy.

I made my down the dock and stared out into the distance. The shoreline across the lake was mostly trees and cabins and houses up on the hills. In Duluth, Lake Superior was so big it was hard to see across. This felt more intimate, friendlier. I was starting to adjust to this small lake town.

A male voice yelled from somewhere behind me, "Hope, Hope!"

No one was in sight until a dog came running at full speed down the dock toward me. I got to my feet as quickly as I could, but it was too late. The dog jumped up on me and I lost my balance. I held on to the dog to lessen its fall with my body.

Before I crashed into the lake, I heard Troy's voice. "Stop! No, Hope, no!"

I landed on my back in the water and cried out in surprise at the cold water. Hope's claws dug into my chest with the impact. The frightened dog yelped and doggy paddled to shore.

Coughing and choking on the water, I said, "Puppy, are you okay?"

Loud footsteps raced across the dock. I looked up to see Troy leaning over with his hand out. I stood in water up to my ribs and rubbed my eyes and squeezed water out of my hair.

Troy held onto a pole on the dock and reached for me. "Are you okay? Let me pull you out."

"I'm fine. I think your dog was excited."

His eyes softened. "Yeah, I'm so sorry about that. Hope rarely does that. I think she really likes you."

"Everyone likes me," I said sarcastically. "It's not usually until the second time I see them that they pounce, so this is a first for me."

He laughed.

What was I saying? I had a habit of making bad jokes when I was nervous. My bad jokes were much better than my social anxiety and awkwardness. I cleared my throat.

"And how often do you have a handsome stranger save you from the cold, dark waters?"

My eyes widened, and I laughed lightly. "I don't know if I'd call you handsome, but I wouldn't call you ugly either."

He tilted his head and looked at me with curiosity. "Oh, thanks. You're full of compliments, aren't you?"

I reached out for his hand and placed my feet on the side of the dock as he pulled me up, his eyes on my wet scrubs. I should have worn a thicker bra today.

That's when I decided to push him into the water, but he grabbed onto the pole like an acrobat, swung around, and landed in the same spot. I groaned. "You have to be kidding me. What were you? A gymnast?"

He gave me a mischievous smile with a glint in his eyes. "You almost got me. Next time, you should probably be sure before you push me in. If you weren't already wet, you'd be in the water by now."

I put my hands on my hips. "I think you already did that." I looked down at my soaking wet clothes.

One side of his mouth curved back into a smirk. "I did no such thing."

Hope walked up the dock all innocent, and stopped

beside her owner. Her tongue hung out of her mouth as she panted.

"Here's the culprit now," he said.

She barked and remained sitting on her hind legs.

"Hope, how dare you take his side?"

Hope put her nose to the dock and yelped with a slight whine.

I put my hands on my knees and bent down to look her in the eye. "Why do I feel bad? You pushed me into the lake, girl."

He squatted down to pat Hope's head. "Because she's so dang cute. Aren't you, girl? You can get away with anything. Can't you?"

Her tail started wagging, and my heart melted. Dogs were my weakness.

"Now, let's get this pretty girl a towel." His eyes lifted to meet mine, and he seemed shocked at his own words.

"That's the least you could do."

"How about dinner at Bimbos as my apology?"

"That's the least you could do," I said, reaching over to pet the dog. "Aren't you just the sweetest thing?"

As if on cue, she shook her body, water flying off her and hitting me in the face.

I wiped my face off with my hands. "I guess I'll need a shower first. How about I walk over after?"

"I'd say make sure you use soap. You kind of smell like a wet dog. Doesn't she, girl?"

I shook my head and walked away. "I'll get my own towel, thanks," I mumbled under my breath.

After an exhausting day, I somehow had energy. Everyone was enjoying the fish fry and here I was out with Troy on a not date. I was hungry, and the restaurant was full but not packed. My brother had told me on the weekends Bimbos was so packed, pizzas took a long time to get done.

Troy looked me over. "Did you warm up?"

"I still feel a bit chilled. I think Hope has it out for me."

"She likes you and she just wanted to mess with you. She rarely jumps on people like that unless she really likes you."

"So I should be grateful."

"Exactly."

I bit my lip. "What's good here?"

"Everything," he said, putting down the menu. "I always pick up the menu, but I always get the same thing."

"What's that?"

"The Big Sturgeon, it's the best burger I ever had. Everyone gives me crap because Bimbos is known for their wings and pizza and sometimes I'll have the pizza, but I'm more of a burger guy."

"That looks massive. Maybe I'll try the Little Sturgeon then. I'd hate to miss out on a big juicy burger."

We both ordered root beer floats to go with our burgers. "This is such a family friendly restaurant. I love it here."

"Let me show you something," he said, getting to his feet. He took my hand and led me to the arcade hidden in the back corner.

We took turns racing, and I played old school Pacman. He won a couple rubber ducks after I told him they would be fun for decorations on Tim's bathtub. I hadn't laughed that hard in so long. We got back to our seats just as the burgers were being placed on the table.

"Anything else I can get for you?" the waiter said.

We both shook our heads and bit into our burgers.

"So tell me about your family," Troy said. "I know Tim,

but I want to hear more about your family. Any embarrassing stories you can tell me about Tim so I can tease him?"

I laughed. "Tim was always the popular kid. He was the only boy in a house with five sisters, including myself. He's one of the kindest people I know, but he comes off a bit cocky at times. I can't think of any embarrassing stories off the top of my head."

"What you're saying is he was a ladies' man? You know he used to date my niece. I should have kicked the crap out of him."

His sarcasm had me grinning. "Out of all my siblings, I'm the only one who got married. Tim and my ex were really close, best friends, actually. My sisters live all over the northern part of the state, but we don't get together often."

"Really? Where do they live? Do they ever visit Tim? He's never said anything about his sisters visiting."

I took another bite of my burger. "Yeah, I'm not sure anyone has been here to visit yet. Actually, I'm pretty sure they haven't. We usually all go to Duluth to my parents' house when we get together. We aren't as close as we should be. We just kind of all went in different directions. My parents have a big house and room for all of us and they make sure we get together a few times a year. As for the rest of my sisters, listen carefully, because I'll quiz you later."

He rubbed his hands together. "Okay, I got this."

"Viv lives in Duluth on the west side. Charlee lives on the Northshore. Miley lives in Tower, and Darci lives in Grand Rapids on Lake Pokegama."

"Do all your siblings live on the lake?"

"Miley does. She lives on Daisy Bay. Charlee lives on Lake Superior and I already told you Darci does, and so does Tim, obviously."

"I guess you guys were all raised on Lake Superior, so you are all drawn to the lake, huh?"

I smiled. "Yeah, I guess we are."

"And all your siblings are living the single life."

I tilted my head. "As far as I know. Milee is always in a relationship, but they never last. She's a web designer, and she does really well for herself. She's very independent and never wants to rely on a man."

"And Viv? Is that short for Vivian?"

I nodded. "She's a free spirit, tends to choose the jerks. She owns a restaurant in Duluth. She's too busy and hasn't even tried to meet anyone. I think she's married to her job. Now Charlee loves the outdoors and is a nanny for some very rich people in a huge house. You need a lot of money to live on the Northshore. She loves children and lives in the family's mansion. She likes to hike and is always in the woods when she isn't working. I know she'd love it here."

"I bet she would. They sure have beautiful waterfalls and trails over there. I love to go fishing on the Northshore. Such a rural area."

"I've always wanted to learn how to fish, but I just never have. I sure love eating fish, though."

"One more sister."

"Darci. She's a probation officer over in Grand Rapids. She was a big trouble maker when we were younger. I always expected her to end up in rehab or something, but she straightened up her act and seems happy. I don't know, she kind of does her own thing. I don't hear from her much."

I looked into his eyes, trying to read his thoughts. "And that's my family."

"That's a big family," he said.

I loudly sipped up my root beer float and Troy joined me until the surrounding tables started staring.

"We should probably stop," I said with a laugh.

He slurped two more times, each one louder. "Nah, let's give them something to talk about."

"Now tell me about your family," I said.

"That's for another day. I already mentioned I didn't have the best upbringing. My parents were doctors but my father loved us with his fists. It wasn't a very health relationship."

"That's terrible."

"It's funny how people look the other way or don't want to believe it when your parents are doctors. I think that's why Kevin and I are so close and why he became a police officer. He wanted to help people who might be in a similar situation."

My eyes widened. "I had no idea. That's so honorable of him."

He nodded. "But that's a bit heavy for our first non-date. Thank you for listening."

I put my hand over his on the table. "Any time. Thank you for sharing that with me. I'm sure it wasn't easy."

He just smiled back and wiped his lips with his napkin. "You are a breath of fresh air, Ima. You know that?"

I was unsure exactly what he meant but I liked his words. I wasn't going to press it any further.

Chapter 17

Lizzy

The sun woke me, and I hopped out of bed. Today was the day Troy was taking me to solve the mystery of the key Victoria left for me. Why would she leave the key to me if there was nothing to find? The key definitely looked like a PO Box key, but then again, I'd never really seen them before. I knew they were small, and that was all I knew. The key did not have a number on it, so I was not sure if Troy was right.

I walked into the kitchen, and Troy was leaning over the stove, flipping a piece of bread. "Hungry?"

"You're in a good mood. What did you make? French toast?"

"I thought it would be a pleasant start to our day. I'm as curious as you are to find out what that key is for. I'm still convinced it's a PO Box key. Maybe Side Lake, Chisholm or even Hibbing. Or maybe it's a safe deposit box at our bank or something."

"Great idea. Did you sleep?"

He laughed. "Yes, I did."

"You sure got in late last night. I heard the door shut."

"I had a good time. I went for burgers with Olivia."

I studied his face as I sat down at the counter. "And?"

"And what? We're friends. Stop trying to make it more than it is. I'm married."

"Widowed," I said.

He glared at me. "A widower."

"Sorry. A widower." This felt like progress.

He said nothing, but set the plate of French toast down on the table and sprinkled some powdered sugar on top. He set homemade maple syrup and Ready Whip in front of me.

"You really went all out, you know that? This looks amazing."

And it really was. This was something Aunt Victoria would do for me when she was alive.

We went into the Side Lake post office first.

"Ida," Troy said as he approached an older lady separating mail. "Is this a key for a PO Box?"

She wiped her hands off and took the key from him, examining it. "Nope. Not one of ours. Where did it come from? Did you find it?"

"Victoria gave it to our niece Lizzy before she died, and we don't know what it's for."

"That's too bad. Try Chisholm or Hibbing."

"That's what we're thinking. Thank you for all your help."

The same thing happened in Chisholm and in Hibbing. They all said the same thing. No, it was not a key to their mailboxes.

"Bank?" Troy said as we pulled out of the Hibbing post office.

"Must be. I don't know what else it could be for."

We pulled into the parking lot of Security State Bank.

"This is the only other place I think she would have a key. She loved her small-town bank. This place has always been very good to us."

We walked inside and I was pleasantly surprised to see how nice it looked.

A lady sitting at a desk to our left stood up. "Welcome to Security. How can I help you?" She batted her eyelashes at Troy and tried not to make it obvious as she eyed him up.

"I'm just wondering if my wife had a security deposit box. You see, she passed away and left us this key, but never told us what it was for."

She took the key from Troy's hand and examined it in the same way all the ladies at the post offices did.

"I'm so sorry for your loss, sir. I'm not sure if this is one of our keys or not. What is her name—was her name?" She seemed a little nervous, and she was blushing.

Troy did not notice. He told the woman Victoria's name and spelled it for her. She typed away on her keyboard and then looked up.

"I'm sorry. She has nothing with us here other than your checking and savings accounts. Have you tried any other banks?"

He shook his head. "No, it would only be this one. This was her favorite bank. No matter where we traveled in the world, this was the only bank she said she wanted. You guys did so much for our family. Thank you for your time."

"You're welcome, sir. I hope you find what you are looking for," she said with a warm smile.

We got back into the car, and I lost it. I laughed until I had tears in my eyes. Troy just stared at me.

"Really? Why are you laughing?" He shifted in his seat

and frowned. "There's nowhere else I can think of. What's so funny? Did I miss something?"

"Uncle Troy, you're really dense. Aren't you?"

He blinked. "What do you mean? I think I missed something here."

I wiped the tears from under my eyes. "That woman was so into you and she felt so guilty about it after you disclosed your wife passed."

He wrinkled his brow. "That's why you're laughing?"

"I'm laughing because you're oblivious to how handsome you are. It's cute. That woman was hot, and you didn't even notice how nervous she got around you. Did you?" I raised my eyebrows at him.

He gave me the look of death. If his eyes could kill. "I guess not. I was too busy thinking about my wife and what this damn key is for."

I leaned over and pinched his cheek, and he pinched mine back. He finally joined in the laughter until his laughs subsided and turned to tears.

"I didn't mean to upset you, Uncle Troy. Are you okay?"

He shook his head and wiped his eyes. "It's hard to imagine living in a world where the love of my life doesn't exist and I have to keep living without her. Sometimes it feels like a dream that she's gone. I miss her. It's just not right. We were supposed to live the rest of our lives together."

Now I was crying. I pointed at my eyes. "Look what you're making me do now. I think we need a distraction. Let's get a bottle of wine and some beer and go back to your house and search for some kind of lock box in your house. It has to be there."

He bit his lip. "I have a better idea, lets invite everyone over to look with us. We'll make a night out of it."

"That sounds like the perfect plan. We should probably pick up some pizza before we head out."

"What do you have in mind?" he said.

I pointed across the street. "I hear Rudi's has great pizza and even better subs. Let's do a group text and see what everyone wants."

"That's going to take a while, but I'm in," he said. "Now, you text."

Chapter 18

Olivia

I made my way down to Tim's dock early the next morning to take out the kayak. The chilly morning breeze off the lake went down the back of my sweatshirt and I shivered. Once I got in the kayak and started paddling, I'd warm up fast.

Growing up with my childhood home right on Lake Superior, I would go kayaking early in the year, often paddling around chunks of ice as they broke off in the water. My siblings and I would make a game out of it, seeing how fast we could get around small icefloes. Tim usually won, but we all expected him to. He was the athlete and the guy who made up the game.

Five minutes in sweat was dripping down my back and I was thinking about removing my sweatshirt. The sun began to rise and shone like a spotlight over the lake. The colors of orange, pink, and yellow came from behind the trees at the eastern end of the lake. I slowed the kayak and took a photo of the beautiful scene. This was my first Side Lake sunrise, and I had come out more for the view than the exercise. Wisps of fog floated off the lake, which blurred the colors and made it mystic.

I took in a deep breath and thoughts of the tiny baby growing inside me left me with goosebumps and an elevated heart rate. I was going to be a mother. I needed to say it out loud to believe it. "I'm going to be a mom. Oh my gosh, I'm going to be a mom!" Okay, that might have been a little too loud.

I laughed to myself.

I was having a little baby whom I would love up. I stopped laughing. What if the baby resented me for leaving his or her father? What if I did the wrong thing by divorcing Ben?

My overthinking was taking over and my concerns were spiraling into something more than what they were. I did not even have the baby yet. This couldn't be healthy.

One day at a time.

"I'm going to be a mom. A damn good one."

I turned the kayak around and paddled back to Tim's.

Knuckles tapped on my bedroom door. What time was it? How long had I been sleeping?

"Come in," I said.

Tim peeked his head around the door. "I was wondering if you fell asleep. I heard the shower running earlier, so I know you've been up."

I sat up and rubbed my eyes. "I took your kayak out and when I got back I was so exhausted, I showered and passed out. What time is it?"

"It's close to dinnertime."

"I guess I was tired."

"I'm sorry I woke you, but I'm on my way over to Troy's

house. They're having some kind of treasure hunt to find out what some key is for."

I was so confused. "Wait, they're having everyone over to search for something a key fits into."

"Yep. You coming?"

"Is there going to be food?"

"Yes, they send out a text asking what everyone wanted. I ordered for you already."

When we arrived at Troy's house, everyone was wandering through the house. The cushions were torn off the couch, and Brad was knocking on the wall, as if trying to find a secret hiding place. Were they high?

Kevin sat on the floor, trying to pry up the floorboards, with no success. Lyndsey stared at him, her expression confused, while she laughed behind her hand. "Seriously Kevin? You really think she hid something in the floorboards?

Who was she? Victoria? I was still trying to figure out exactly what they were talking about.

Maddy spotted me and her entire face lit up. "Liv! Are you here to help with the hunt?"

I kept watching Kevin. Would he find some kind of wiggly board in the tongue-and-groove flooring? He did not look like he was giving up anytime soon. "What hunt exactly? Something about a key?" I said, looking over at Tim for help.

Maddy smiled. "The Christmas before Victoria passed away, she gave Lizzy a key and never told her what it was for. Lizzy and Troy went to all the surrounding post offices and the bank to figure out what the key was for, but they hit dead ends. Troy thinks whatever the key unlocks is hidden in this house. He says it's the only logical answer."

"I get it now. What can I do to help?"

"There are no rules. Tim, why don't you check the basement? Liv, come upstairs with me. Let's start in Troy's room."

That was the last place I wanted to be, but a part of me wondered what it looked like. My curiosity got the best of me. "Let's go."

"This house was Troy's parents' cabin growing up," Maddy said.

"His cabin?" The judgement seeped into my voice.

The house was massive. No way this place was just a cabin for seasonal use. What a waste. They must have been loaded. Sure, my parents were well off growing up, and we lived in a good- sized mansion on Lake Superior, but it was our home. We lived there all year, and my parents remodeled it with their own bare hands. The house needed work when they bought it, but they made it nice. They even painted the exterior when the paint was peeling off.

I followed Maddy up the stairs and into Troy's room. His bedroom was huge and spotless. He had a jacuzzi tub in the master bathroom with a massive, tinted window behind it. I went over to the walk-in closet and held my breath. Squared shelves lined the back of the closet, filled with women's shoes of all colors and styles, from stilettos to running shoes and fancy boots.

To the left of the closet were men's clothes, color coordinated with a majority of blues and blacks and a shelf with folded sweaters and shoes above it. The right of the closet held women's clothing, also coordinated by color. He had not touched Victoria's clothes since she passed away.

A square in the ceiling above my head distracted me

from my thoughts. I stepped back into the bedroom. "Do you know where Troy keeps his ladder?" I pointed up at the ceiling behind me and her eyes opened wide with excitement.

"I'm not sure. I know he's in the basement, if you want to ask him. If he doesn't have one, I can have Brad run home and get ours."

I nodded and made my way downstairs. I rounded the corner, in search of the way to the basement, when I saw him sitting on the floor in the living room with a box open in front of him.

"Hey, Troy?"

He turned toward me with a huge smile on his face.

His smile was so charming, it erased my thoughts. What had I come to ask him again?

I made my way to his side. "You look happy. Did you find something?" I peeked my head over the box, trying to see what it was that made him so happy.

"It's kind of funny. Every now and then, I find something Victoria left for me. A month after she passed, I got a letter in the mail thanking me for my donation to the National Coalition Against Domestic Violence."

"Because of your parents," I said. It wasn't a question. I knew from what he told me, his father abused him.

"Yeah."

Our eyes met, and my lungs collapsed at the thought.

"Then, a few months later, I found a note inside my pillow. I was taking my pillowcase off to wash it and here was this pink note inside that said, "It's about time you stopped sulking and washed these sheets.""

I laughed sympathetically. She wanted to make sure he got himself back up and into a routine after she passed. She cared more about him than herself. That was obvious.

"Once I found that note, I started looking for more notes. I found one in the garage telling me it was about time I cleaned the garage and next I should redo the basement the way I wanted. She was always like that. Selfless, and wanting to take care of me. Even when she was sick, she was planning to help us all deal with her being sick."

He shook his head. "I just found this box full of funny quotes and this note." He passed it over to me. "Before she passed, she told me when Lizzy started asking about the key or if she was engaged to open this box and I forgot about it until we left the bank. Here, read this."

Troy,

This box is full of quotes to make you laugh and a very important letter for Lizzy. I'm worried about her. Although she seems happy with Tim, I can see she is slowly pulling away from her relationship with him. Although I love my sister dearly, she hasn't really been a mom for Lizzy, and I know I need to step up. Since I'm not around to do it myself, this obligation is now yours. You're welcome. Hear me out.

I gave Lizzy a key for Christmas and I've avoided the questions about what it is for. I don't want you to tell her what it unlocks until the time is right. I'll explain—since you are a man and probably need a little extra explanation (I love you but you know it's true!) I need you to share this letter with someone you trust, someone you know who knows Lizzy well enough to help you on this secret mission. Someone outside our friend group would be a bonus.

.   .   .

You and I had the most wonderful marriage. You are and will always be my best friend. It didn't start off that way, though. Did it? It was hard, and we had a lot of fights and I ran away and you struggled with giving me space. There were days I didn't know if we would make it through and there were days our passion was so strong I thought we could never be apart.

It took me a long time to understand your reactions were due to what your father did to your family growing up. No child should ever have to endure what you and your brother went through. It hurt my heart so much to see the way he treated you and your mother, even when you were an adult. I also saw the way it broke you and Kevin both when he died. I still really didn't understand the mental effects of abuse until I saw the way your mother broke after he passed. I thought she would be happy, but instead she struggled more.

Lizzy struggled with the emotional abuse and neglect growing up. A mother who was a chronic alcoholic and a father who passed away too young. You get her like no one else could, and that's why it's so important you're the one to help her. Be there for her when her heart breaks and be her support. Watch her fall in love and let her know it's okay. Tell her you understand and don't let her give up on love. I'd like to say Tim is the person for her and they really are amazing together, aren't they? But I know only Lizzy can make that choice. I know she will find herself someday, and I just hope she does before it's too late. I have complete trust in you. You've got this. She just needs the guidance, love, and support to love herself so she can be happy and let herself fall in love with the right person. Dalton really broke her, and I can see the fear in her eyes that it will happen again.

Once she falls in love, it'll be time to find the treasure that is hidden at the highest level. I love you so much and I always will. You've got this.

Love you,
Victoria

Chapter 19

Lizzy

I ran up the stairs. "Uncle Troy, where are you?" He had been looking through the pantry in the basement when a look of revelation crossed his face. He'd disappeared upstairs.. I searched through every inch of the basement with the help of Brad, Kevin, and Ethan before I finally gave up. Whatever the key opened was not down there.

I heard some movement in the living room and saw Olivia jump to her feet.

"I'm here," Troy said.

He looked guilty or suspicious, but I would not push it or bring attention to how excited I was to see him in deep conversation with Olivia. Maybe it was nothing, but he seemed to smile more when she was around.

"It's definitely not in the basement. Did you guys find anything in here?"

They shook their heads, but they both looked guilty.

"Nope. I just came across some old things I was showing Olivia here. I don't think whatever that key unlocks is here. We should just throw in the towel and go sit down by the lake and relax. What do you think?"

He was right. "I agree. It's beautiful out there."

The answer to the key was not in the house. Maybe I'd never know what the key was for. Maybe the key wasn't really for anything anymore. Maybe the key itself meant something to Victoria, like a good luck charm. I might never find out and I was okay with that because every time I looked at it I thought of her and what was better than that?

Whitney and Josh insisted we head to their house because it was on Side Lake. They had a sandy beach in front of their place and a pontoon that could fit us all. Their daughter Brittany was already playing in the sand and little David, Maddy and Brad's son, came running up to help her build a sandcastle.

I looked over at Olivia standing beside me and, just as expected, she had a smile from ear to ear that lit up her face as she watched the kids get excited about the size of their sandcastle.

Olivia joined the kids. "You guys need any help?"

"Yeah!"

They were excited for an adult to pay attention to them while they were working so hard to build what Brittany called, "The biggest sandcastle ever!"

I helped Kat lay out a giant beach blanket on the sand. Brad and Kevin brought chairs over to sit in. Tim sat beneath the shadow of the tree. He was watching his sister dig in the sand to create a body of water surrounding the castle.

"I think you guys need some help from a professional," he said, rolling up his sleeves. He walked over to the tree just behind us and started breaking off small branches. He brought them over and laid them down next to that castle.

Brittany stopped building to watch him work. "What's that for, Uncle Tim?"

"This is for the bridge, so the people in the castle can get over the water."

"That's awesome!" David said.

They were just about finished with their sandcastle when a giant wave from a boat passing by came crashing onto the shore and the sandcastle vanished. All that was left was one lump of the castle and a couple of sticks from the bridge.

"Oh, no! It's gone," Brittany said. Her lip jutted out in an impressive pout.

"I think that means it's the perfect time to take the pontoon out. What do you think?" Josh said to the kids.

Brittany and David looked at each other with excited little faces.

David squealed. "Can we, mom? Can we? Please!"

"I don't see why not," Maddy said, looking at Brad to make sure he agreed.

He nodded. "Sounds good to me."

"Why doesn't everyone get in the boat? I just need to grab something quick," Josh said. He looked at Kevin and Brad. "Can you two help me carry something?"

"I'll grab the towels," Whitney said. "Kids, get your life jackets on."

They jumped up and ran as fast as they could, racing to the pontoon.

Minutes later, the guys came back carrying a giant blowup of some sort. I leaned forward and pulled my sunglasses down to see better.

Tim stood up. "Is that a giant slide?"

"It's a pontoon zip slide," Brad said as they carried it up the dock and attached it to the back of the pontoon

That really made the kids excited. They jumped up and down.

"A slide for the boat! No way! Can I try first, please dad," Brittany said.

"I don't see why not," Whitney said.

"Then me!" David said.

Once they got it attached and it looked to be secure, Josh took the boat into the middle of the lake and shut off the engine. "Okay, guys. Let's see how it works," Josh said.

Brittany was already off her seat and climbing up the slide. She sat down and looked at David. "You ready for this, David?"

He nodded his head dramatically. "Go!"

Brittany slid into the water with a giant splash. Then screamed. "The water is so cold! Burr!"

She swam to the side of the boat, and Tim leaned over the edge to pull her in. "That was so much fun! You have to try it!" Brittany said to no one in particular.

David went in next. The water off Brittany and her life jacket splashed on me, and I pulled my legs into my body to warm up.

"Sorry, Lizzy. I didn't mean to get you all wet," Brittany said.

I smiled at her. "I'm glad you did because now I want to try out your new slide."

She clapped her hands and jumped up and down. Her little ten-year-old arms were bent, and she was hunched over, her teeth chattering. I grabbed a towel and wrapped it around her.

"Really?"

"Really," I said.

Tim jumped up behind me. "I'll go after you."

I looked around the boat. "How am I going to get back in?"

"I'll pull you in," Tim said. His eyes glimmered, and I was immediately skeptical. "I'm not sure I trust you."

Kevin stood up. "I'll help you."

I felt much better about him. Plus, Kevin was a police officer. He was much stronger than Tim, and he was used to saving people.

"Deal," I said.

Tim looked disappointed, but I tried to shake it off. I climbed up the ladder. Every wobbly step made me feel like it was going to collapse. "Are you sure I'm not too heavy?" I asked once I was sitting at the top.

Tim laughed behind me. "If you were too heavy, it would have collapsed before you got to the top."

"Here goes nothing," I said before pushing off. My body hit the water, and the coldness took my breath away. The water was like an ice bath. I grunted the entire way to the side of the boat, my body numb.

I heard a splash, and then Tim was right behind me.

Kevin leaned over the side to pull me up and braced his leg on the side so he wouldn't fall in. Tim helped boost me up from behind as I climbed in. Maddy threw me a towel once I was back in the boat.

Tim climbed in on his own, making it look easy.

"Showoff," I whispered once he was standing beside me.

Ignoring him was getting too difficult. Being myself and not letting him bother me was so much easier. Avoiding him all the time was difficult, and if I kept it up, the summer would be miserable. We had the same friends and were living on the same street again. The only way I would make it through the summer was to stop trying so hard to avoid him. He didn't deserve that, and I was miserable. The truth was, I missed him.

His eyes lit up. "Just wait until you see me wake surf."

Did I hear him right? "Wake surf?"

"I'm not going to lie. It's pretty cool to watch," Olivia said. "My brother has no fear behind a boat."

"You've never heard of wave surfing?" Brad said. "It is harder than hell. But I'm bound and determined to surf longer than this guy this summer." He put his arm around Tim's shoulder.

Tim grinned at me in the way I never could resist. I looked away to break the eye contact, but I had gooscbumps and not from the cold water.

"They pretty much surf right behind the boat, like right behind the boat in the wake, and drop the rope and surf without holding onto anything," Kat said with a groan.

Maddy piped in. "Yeah, and all of us sit there and watch, holding our breath because we are so worried these guys are going to fall and split their damn heads open."

"It's true," Kat said with a laugh. "Well, for me, Maddy, and Victoria anyway. Lyndsey is just as good as the guys and eggs them on."

"Really? Well, if she is anywhere near as good as she is at skiing, I can see that," Olivia said with a squeal in her voice. "I would love to see someone beat my brother at a water sport."

Tim wiped his face with the towel, and for the first time all day, I allowed myself to really look at him. I stared at his eyes and then made my way down his body slowly, with a little extra attention on his torso. That's when I saw him flex his abs and my eyes shot up to his face. He looked away as quickly as he could, but he knew and he saw and I didn't really care. I was done hiding.

Chapter 20

Olivia

By the time we reached Troy's dock, the sun was setting.

"It's so beautiful out here. The moon is so bright it's lighting up the entire sky," I said before stepping off the boat and onto the dock. We had been boating all day and stepping onto solid ground made me feel a bit unstable after being on the boat for so long.

Josh waved as he pulled away in his boat and headed home. Brad carried a sleeping David in his arms. Tim and Lizzy walked in line with Kat and Ethan, while Troy and I trailed behind.

"Meet me on this dock at one o'clock in the morning," he whispered in my ear.

Had I heard him right? "What?"

"Just trust me."

His breath on my ear left me with goosebumps. Why would he want me to meet him on the dock in the middle of the night? But what did I have to lose? Instead of fighting it, I do as he asked. I was curious but I would not ruin the surprise. "One o'clock it is," I said. "What should I wear?"

He laughed. "Something comfortable."

I tried to sleep, but I only tossed and turned, my mind consumed with all the reasons he might want to meet me at one o'clock in the morning. I kept looking at my clock until finally I scrolled social media to distract myself.

I jumped out of bed at 12:45 to brush my teeth and run a brush through my hair, but that was all. I did not want him to think I cared enough to doll myself up to meet him in the middle of the night. He would not see me in the dark, anyway, though the moon was bright.

I had to stop overthinking.

At one o'clock I snuck out the door and made my way to Troy's dock. I was wearing my flannel pjs and a pink and white striped robe. I looked up at the sky for the moon and that was when I realized why he invited me here.

Spotlights illuminated the sky and green reflected off the lake and above the trees. The rest of the sky was lit up bright red. The way the streaks of light were shining, it looked like they were dancing behind the trees. The Northern Lights. He invited me out to see the Northern Lights.

The outline of Troy's body stood tall at the end of the dock. I made my way to his side. "It's beautiful, isn't it?"

The green lights reflected on his face. I laughed.

He turned to me with a confused expression on his face. "What's so funny?"

"You look like the witch from Wicked right now."

He wrinkled his brow, but I could not stop laughing. "It doesn't take much to entertain you, does it?" he said.

I bumped my hand across his arm and it lingered there for a moment more than it should have. That was enough to stop the giggles. "I guess I'm just a little tired. This is absolutely stunning."

He took a deep breath, looked at me, then back at the sky. "I've seen the Northern Lights a million times growing up, but as an adult, I never stayed up to watch them. I guess Victoria and I spent so much time traveling the world, I never stopped and thought about what was here, right in front of me at the place where I grew up."

"I know the feeling." I wrapped my arms around my body. The chilly breeze coming off the water made me shiver. "I've lived in Minnesota my whole life and I've never stayed up to watch the Northern Lights."

He turned to me with a look of amazement written all over his face. "This is your first time?"

How could his basic words make my heart go into overdrive so fast? It had to be the hormones.

The back of his hand brushed against mine until our fingers hung there, touching. I didn't want to pull my hand away. The warmth of his skin against mine took my breath away. The moment was far too romantic to fight. What was he thinking inviting me out here?

"I could stay here all night until the sun comes up," he said.

"I don't think I could. I have to work at seven in the morning.

He deadpanned. "What? Why did you come out here if you had to work so early? You should have told me."

"And miss this?" Our eyes connected. I could not pull my gaze away and the feeling seemed mutual.

"You didn't even know I was bringing you here to see the Northern Lights."

Busted. I nodded. "True, but my curiosity got the best of me.

His fingers were now rubbing mine. I froze in place, unable to move, and focused on his touch. The warmth of his fingers made my whole body crazy. I closed my eyes.

His hand traveled up my back and left a shiver in its path until his hand slid to my arm and he pulled me into his warm body. I rested my head on his shoulder. We both kept looking up at the sky.

Everything about this moment was too perfect to be real. It had to be a dream. He was in love with his deceased wife. Maybe I was taking advantage of him in this moment. Should I walk away? Tell him I was pregnant? That would be sure to make him run in the other direction.

Instead, I let my body turn on its own toward him. My hands lifted to meet behind his neck and we stared into each other's eyes. His hands were now around my waist. We just stared at each other. I leaned in at a snail's pace and he did, too.

We were just a whisper away when we both stopped. I needed him to make the move. For his lips to make those last few inches without my insistence, but after what felt like forever, I opened my eyes to see what the holdup was.

His smile reached my soul, and I smiled right back. I licked my lips, staring at his swollen upper lip.

He leaned his forehead against mine and closed his eyes.

I had to strain my ears to hear his quiet whisper in the night. At first, I wasn't even sure it was real. "Goodnight, Ima."

I opened my eyes, our foreheads still resting together. He pulled away and cupped my face in his hands as he stared into my eyes and at my lips. My heart broke when he turned away.

I stood there, not uttering a sound as I watched him walk up the stairs.

What the hell was that?

I'm not sure how much time passed as I stood there, staring into the distance, unable to catch my breath.

What just happened?

Chapter 21

Lizzy

Where was Olivia? Was she awake? I waited five more minutes in her driveway. I was just about to knock on Tim's door when the outside light turned on and she came running out to the car.

"Sorry I'm late. I had a hard time sleeping."

"You're fine, but you had me worried. I'm glad I didn't have to pound on your door before sunrise."

She seemed frazzled. "It won't happen again."

She was not acting like herself, but I was not about to push it.

We drove most of the way in silence, but when we got to work, I noticed the dark circles under her eyes. "Everything okay, Lizzy? You don't look real good. I know you didn't sleep well, but you look a little pale."

She waved me off. "I'm fine. I stayed up to see the Northern Lights. And I have a lot on my mind. Maybe I didn't think this work thing through. I haven't found an obstetrician yet, and I'm a little worried I should have waited until after the baby was born to go back to work."

"When are you due?"

Her body tensed. I reached to open up the hospital doors, and her eyes stared at the ground.

"I'm not actually sure. I haven't seen a doctor yet."

"Are you kidding me? Why?"

She grabbed my hand and pulled me into the bathroom down the hall and shut the door. "I know, I know. I'm on prenatal vitamins and I have taken five pregnancy tests, so I know I'm pregnant and I'm eating very healthy, but as soon as I found out, that ended Ben and me."

"Why?"

"Ben has been cheating on me for years, and as soon as I found out I left him. I don't want my family to know and I don't want Tim to know. He'd probably kill Ben."

"Wait, that doesn't make sense. Unless... Is the baby his?"

"We had one last hurrah, and I ended up pregnant. I moved to Duluth soon after and then Side Lake." She bit on her nail and looked away. "My guess is I'm somewhere in my second trimester."

"What about your period?"

"It's always light."

How could she procrastinate? She was a nurse. A nurse who worked on the maternity floor. She knew the risks of not being under a doctor's care. This was reckless, but was it really my place? Yes, it was. She needed someone to talk some sense into her.

I let out a loud exhale. "Listen, I know one of the best OB-GYN's on the Iron Range. I've worked with her enough to know how good she is. She fights hard for her patients. She may give you a lecture for waiting this long, but you and your baby will be in great hands."

She nodded. "Thanks, Lizzy. Hey, one last thing."

I pursed my lips. "Anything."

"Will you come to my first visit with me?"

She wanted me there with her? I was touched. "I wouldn't miss it." I gave her a tight hug. "Now, we'd better get going or we'll be late and if our favorite doctor is around, we won't hear the end of it."

Dr. Evans was angry, and his tone was sharp and forceful the moment I saw him. He was lecturing his patient, and I could tell the minute he looked at me with furrowed brows I was going to be his target today.

"I don't care what we discussed regarding your birth plan. I'm not taking risks. If there are complications, I will do what is necessary. Unless you have been to medical school, you need to listen to me. No more arguing or you can find yourself another doctor," he told the woman.

Boy, was it hard for me to bite my tongue. How would she find another doctor? She was in labor right now.

No matter what I did, he was riding me. I took Andrea's vitals, she was a thirty-seven-year-old, and therefore; considered advanced maternal age and a high-risk pregnancy.

Dr. Evans kept calling her a geriatric pregnancy, which is insensitive and outdated. Let alone the fact that he never addressed her by name was concerning. If he was going to treat me disrespectfully, I could handle that. But if he treated a woman in labor that way, I could not keep my mouth shut. I was officially an RN and that meant something to me. My patients meant more to me than that. If he kept up his disrespectful attitude toward Andrea, I was going to lose it on him.

I put a smile on my face and tried to lighten Andrea's mood. I hooked up her iPhone to a speaker and played her favorite music to help her stay calm. I could see the heartbreak in her eyes every time the doctor put her down and talked about her condition like she was not in the room.

Good thing Olivia was not in the room or she would probably end up fired. She was not afraid to go toe-to-toe with Dr. Evans like the rest of us.

Once he left the room, I got Andrea some ice chips and set them on the table next to her.

"How are you doing? Can I get you anything else? Are you in any pain right now?"

Her eyes were still glossy with tears from the last contraction. "My husband should be here already. He was supposed to land twenty minutes ago."

I patted her arm. "He'll get here. You've got time."

"I don't mean to sound like a complainer, but my doctor is an absolute jerk. I wish I listened to my husband and gone with someone else." She looked into my eyes. "I'm not even forty years old. Why does he keep saying my baby is high risk and I should be prepared for a c-section because there is no way I'm having this baby vaginally? Is my baby going to be okay?"

She was panicking now and pulling on my arm. Her heartbeat was picking up pace. She needed to calm down. The baby was going to be in distress if she didn't relax.

"Look at me, okay?"

She nodded and stared into my eyes.

"Your husband is going to walk through that door any moment and you're going to feel so much better. Dr. Evans is just preparing in case anything were to go wrong. He does that with every patient because he always wants to be prepared. He does not mean to scare you, he's just thorough. You hear me?"

She kept nodding. Her hand squeezed mine tight as she braced herself and grunted in pain.

"Breathe, breathe, okay? Look at me and breathe with me."

She copied my breathing until her body relaxed.

"Thank you," she said.

"I've had many patients your age or older having babies here, and so many have had natural births. Don't you worry about that. Everything is going to be okay. If it comes to a c-section, you're in the best of hands. Everything is going to be okay."

"Thank you. What's your name?"

I smiled. "Lizzy. And if you need anything, even just a hand to hold, you push that button right there, okay?"

"Okay."

"Now, give me your phone. I'm calling your husband again."

Thirty minutes later, her husband was by her side. He apologized and rubbed her feet, held her hand through the contractions, and puffed out his chest when Dr. Evans came in and told him it was about time he showed up.

Evans was on my last nerve. I had to walk away just to calm down. I went to the nurse's station and worked on my charting. I was only there for a few minutes when Adam called me into his office and shut the door.

"You okay? You look a bit overwhelmed."

I blinked away the tears. I would not let a bully like Dr. Evans know he got to me.

"I'm fine."

He raised his eyebrows at me. "I know you better than that, Lizzy."

I crossed my arms and looked out the window. If I

talked too much, I was afraid I'd lose control of my emotions.

"It's okay if you don't want to talk about it. Just tell me one thing."

I looked into his eyes.

"Is it Dr. Evans again?"

I did not need to say anything. He knew right away. He let out a deep exhale, ran his fingers through his hair, and hung his head. He turned his back to me and looked out the window, silent for a minute. He finally turned around with a look of defeat and concern written all over his face. "I feel like a failure. I've tried talking to the board, I've talked to him, but my hands are tied here. He's just a miserable old man who's ready to retire. I'm sorry I can't do more."

His words were genuine. Adam cared deeply for all his nurses, and I knew he had no control in the matter. There wasn't much he could do. I just needed to learn to deal with it. Dr. Evans would not leave Virginia, and he was not that close to retirement. I had to suck it up and deal with it.

I stood up. "Adam, I know you are doing everything you can, but we both know there's really nothing you can do. I appreciate you and all you do. You're a wonderful supervisor and a big part of the reason I wanted to work on the maternity floor as an RN."

I had a feeling he was the reason I got on staff so quickly. Usually a nurse needed a lot of experience before working on the maternity floor. My gut told me he fought to get me here.

I put my hand on his shoulder as I turned to open the door. "Thank you for caring and trying to help. I won't let an ignorant doctor ruin my day. I've worked so hard to get where I am, and I'm so grateful to be here. I just needed a break, and that was exactly what you gave me. Thank you, Adam."

He grabbed my arm, and I did not fight him as he pulled me into him. I couldn't move. I stared at him, unsure of what he would do next. My heart raced. Our faces were an inch or two apart and we stared at each other, neither of us making the next move. I knew he wanted to, but he let me go instead.

He was my supervisor. We both knew nothing could happen between us. I walked away with a bounce in my step, and I held my shoulders back and my head up before walking into Andrea's room with another cup of ice chips in my hand.

Chapter 22

Olivia

"I can't believe he talked to her like that. That's terrible." Lizzy just nodded. "I won't let him get to me anymore. I'm not scared of him."

I reached across the armrest of the car and squeezed her hand. "Good for you. He's an overweight, miserable old man who talks down to pregnant women and nurses. Maybe his wife is Satan or something. He's not worth it. He probably gets punished enough at home."

"His wife actually works on our floor, and she's really nice. I think, if anything, he's like that to her, too. But enough about that jerk. How was your day, Liv? I feel like I hardly saw you at all."

I smiled. "It was good. I'm just tired. I called Dr. Abby's office and made an appointment today."

"I'm so proud of you."

Lizzy and I visited the OB-GYN the following week, and I finally had a due date.

Tim was mowing the lawn when Lizzy dropped me off. He shut off the mower and wiped away the sweat on his face with his forearm.

"No need to stop on my behalf," I said.

He followed me inside. "I needed a glass of water, anyway. How did the doctor visit go? Did you like Dr. Abby?"

"Yeah, and I've a due date."

He chugged his glass of water. "Oh?"

"It's October thirty-first."

He put his empty glass down on the counter, his eyes open wide. "No shit. Halloween? That's a big party on its own. So, you're a little further along than you expected."

The sharp pain in my back and legs hit me at once, and I winced in pain.

"Sit down, Liv. Your long work hours are hard on your body. Are you sure you want to work right now? You're carrying another person in there, you know."

I rolled my eyes at him. "Such a man. How am I supposed to pay my bills and take some time off after the baby is born if I don't work now?"

He put his hands on my shoulders. "Listen to me, Liv. Let me help you. You got money for the house sale, right? You have plenty of money, and I want to help, too. Let me throw you a baby shower."

My chin dropped. "You throw me a baby shower?"

"What's wrong with that? Is there some rule against your brother throwing you a baby shower?"

I squinted at him.

"Okay, I'll probably ask our friends for some help, but I want to do this. Let me."

His offer was so sweet, and I really wanted to celebrate

this little baby growing inside me. "I'd like that. Why don't you have Lizzy help you?"

"Lizzy?" he said, as if he didn't know who she was.

"Yes, Lizzy. You know, the girl you go all google eyed for every time you see her."

He frowned. "I do not."

"Yes, you do, but so does she."

His posture stiffened. "She does?"

I knew it. They still had feelings for each other. "Yes, she does. I don't know how you don't see it."

"It doesn't matter. She doesn't want to be with me."

"Tim, if there was a tiny spark left for Ben, I'd be in London trying to win him back in a heartbeat. We had fun, but we never had much in common. The beginning was exciting, but when he and I split up, I never felt more relieved. Ask yourself, do you want to be with her? Is life better or worse without her? Will you regret it if you don't chase after her?'

He covered his face with his hands. When he pulled them away, his face was a dark shade of red. "You don't get it, Liv. She doesn't want to be with me. I've tried everything. She asked me to stay away from her. I've never felt this way about a woman before. I'm so madly in love with her I can't even sleep without dreaming about her. If there was anything at all I could do to win her back, I'd do it, but I'm so damn afraid that no matter what I do, it'll push her away even more."

I took a step toward him, and he backed away. I had not realized he felt this deeply. I knew they liked each other and I could see the chemistry, but I'd never seen my brother fall this hard for a woman. He never liked to talk about his relationships. "Don't lose hope. She'll be back. I just know she will."

The guilt consumed me. I'd pushed her toward Adam. But in the end, whatever was meant to be would be. It was not my place to get involved.

The next week was filled with thunderstorms and lots of rain. Tim said the rain was good because the water levels were low and he was worried about the boat making it through the channel. It got stuck every time we went from Little Sturgeon to Big Sturgeon, and the guys had to push. Brad said there was too much weight, but Tim said it would happen, anyway. Although we had a lot of snow over the winter, it had not rained in a while. We often took out Josh's pontoon because it did not have a large prop to hit bottom, like the wakeboard boat.

The rain finally stopped toward the end of June. I was looking forward to the Fourth of July the following week. Everyone told me it was the best day of the year in Side Lake. We all signed up for the Firecracker 5k in Side Lake, and we were decorating the float for the parade this week. Most of us would head to Riverside for the adult party while Maddy, Brad, Whitney, and Josh would go to Bimbos because they had a big celebration for the kids every year with bouncy houses and lots of games. For such a small town, I could not believe all the events they held.

I had not worked with Dr. Evans much the past couple of weeks, which made work easier.

On a break, I ran to the cafeteria to get some food. I forgot to pack myself a lunch, and I never ate much when I worked because I was always so busy I'd forget. But now that I was pregnant, I was hungry all the time. And tired. So tired all the time.

Adam was getting a tray as I made my way through the food line. He nodded for me to join him at a table in the corner, and I did.

"How are you doing, Olivia? You liking it here?"

I took a bite of my apple and nodded. "Yeah. It's a nice hospital, but a lot smaller than the one I worked at in the Cities, but I like it. A lot of skilled nurses."

"Agreed."

The table shook from his knee, bouncing under the table. Something was definitely bothering him, and he looked as though he was afraid to ask me something.

"Listen, I really hope I'm not wrong here or I'm about to humiliate myself."

Now he really caught my attention.

He cleared his throat and then looked at my fingers. "You're retaining water, you have circles under your eyes, your scrubs are a size too big, and there's a hint of a bump." He stopped himself. Obviously nervous to offend me.

"If you are asking if I'm pregnant, I am."

His eyes widened, and he leaned back in his chair. "I'm so glad you said that. I was worried I might be wrong, and I didn't want to offend you."

I laughed and took another loud bite of my apple.

"Why didn't you tell me? Does anyone else know?"

"I told HR when I was hired, but asked them to keep it quiet until I was ready. The only other person who knows at work is Lizzy."

"I figured she did," he said. "She's always looking at you with concern in her eyes. The two of you are close, huh?"

Was he trying to get information from me? He truly was smitten with her. I teased him. "What's it to you?"

His cheeks blushed. "I'm.... I'm...just glad you have someone."

His always steady hands were shaking as he picked up his bottle of water.

"Listen, I'm thinking about taking some time off. You're right, my ankles are swollen and these long hours on my feet are making my ankles look more like cankles."

He laughed and shook his head at my joke.

"Please, just take care of Lizzy while I'm gone. I worry about her. Dr. Evans has been so horrible lately, and I don't want her to get burned out. Being an RN is a tough job. Don't let him scare her away."

"I agree."

I wanted to push him away from Lizzy because I was rooting for her to be with my brother, but I had no choice. Her happiness was the most important thing right now, and she needed to make that decision on her own. Adam was a great person. His kindness was rooted deep.

His eyes softened. "I'm keeping a close eye on Dr. Evans. You nurses don't deserve his abuse. You don't need to worry about Lizzy. I'm doing everything I can to keep her safe."

"Thank you." He was definitely smitten.

Chapter 23

Lizzy

I worked a double since Liv and I didn't ride to work together today. I needed the money, but I was sad to miss the float decorating. Olivia told me she spoke with Adam about taking some time off until the baby was born. I was glad because she was exhausted and I worried about her all the time. Sometimes we did not get a break all day, and I was concerned she would end up dehydrated and pass out or something.

Adam left work around five o'clock, leaving Tanya, Beth, Lucy, and me on duty. The night was quiet. We only had one mother in labor, but she was only dilated to three centimeters and her labor had not progressed in five hours. At ten o'clock, she finally delivered the baby. Dr. Evans said little and seemed to be a little more professional. He did not look my way once, but I was okay with that. He'd talk at me, not to me, but the expecting mother and father did not seem to notice.

"It's a boy!" Dr. Evans said.

He held up the baby for the new parents to see, and

then we began assessing the baby. Beth was helping to train me in assessment. She left to check on a new patient in the next room. I was so emotional when that little boy cried for the first time. Birth was such a beautiful and miraculous experience I still could not wrap my mind around.

The birth was exciting and stressful, but when that baby was born and crying, I finally was able to calm myself down. So much could go wrong, and I was relieved when the baby looked healthy. Being at a smaller hospital, we did not have a NICU if something were to happen.

The baby was crying and seemed to be doing well. He was pink, warm, and crying. He was with the doctor and still crying when I turned around to write the ARGAR score of nine. Only, instead of writing down the baby's vitals and ARGAR score, I heard a loud thud that vibrated in my head, and I lost my breath.

At first I thought he had dropped the baby, but my lungs collapsed with a sudden pain.What just happened? My shoulder stung and my arm went numb. I turned around in confusion.

Dr. Evans said to the father, "Administration expects these damn nurses to document immediately." He snarled at me. "Don't turn your back to me." His words came out as a warning, but the damage was already done.

Did he just hit me?

My mouth hung open in shock. I looked over at the father and his eyes were open wide with surprise.

I cleaned up the room and helped the new mom, Trina, get dressed so she could be more comfortable. I did not stop to think about what happened until I left the patient's room and went into the bathroom. I was confused and embarrassed. Did that really just happen?

The bathroom door opened and Lucy, one of my favorite nurses, peeked her head in.

"Oh, I didn't know you were in here. You forgot to lock the door." She stopped and shut the bathroom door and locked it behind her. "Are you okay?"

I shook my head. "I don't think so."

"What happened?"

"Doctor Evans hit me."

"What? What do you mean, he hit you?"

I told her what happened, and she just stared at me. "Are you sure?"

"Am I sure? Lucy, he punched me in the back when I turned around. I'm absolutely sure."

Was I?

"I mean, I know he can be a jerk, but I don't think he'd actually hit you."

Lucy was an older nurse, just a few years away from retirement. I knew her pretty well from working here, but I did not expect this reaction from her.

"Fine. Let me out," I said, walking around her and opening up the door.

I spent the last couple of hours of my shift charting and organizing, doing my rounds, and checking vitals. I avoided all the nurses. When the next shift arrive, I was getting ready to leave when Dr. Evans stopped me.

"I'm sorry I hit you," he said without any emotion in his tone. "Last weekend, I had a really stressful delivery, and I was a bit hyper vigilant. I overreacted and I'm sorry about that. But you don't document until the doctor tells you to."

Was this an apology or a lecture? I could not believe what I was hearing. Was this his way of apologizing to me?

I just stared at his back as he walked away and out the

main doors. I'm not sure how long I stood there until Tanya came up behind me and put her arm around me. I walked next to her as we left together.

"Hey, I heard what happened and I believe you."

"Yeah," I said.

I felt numb, like a zombie, and so confused. Why would he hit me? What did I do wrong? Should I have done something different? I would not have believed it myself if I hadn't both felt and heard that punch and then the worst apology I'd ever heard. From a professional.

"I want you to know I checked on Trina. Her husband, James, told me he felt terrible because the doctor punched you in the back with his fist. Are you okay?"

I shook my head. "I'm not sure. It's a blur."

"Maybe you want to make a police report?"

I shook my head.

"How about if you call Adam? He'll know what to do."

I nodded. I could do that. My body was weak, and my back was getting sore now that the shock had worn off.

I made a mistake. I never should have become a nurse. Why did I think I could?

"Are you sure you're okay to drive?"

I nodded. "I'm okay."

"Promise me you'll call Adam. It doesn't matter that it's late. Call him. Promise?"

I nodded again.

I got into my car and started it up, then dialed Adam's number. His familiar voice when he answered broke me. I cried so hard, I could not stop.

"Lizzy, are you okay? What happened?"

More crying.

"Where are you?"

I still could not get out any words.

"Are you at the hospital? Are you driving?"

I shook my head, but he could not see me. "I'm in the parking lot. In my car. At the hospital."

"Don't move and whatever you do, do not drive. I'm on my way."

Chapter 24

Olivia

I waited ten minutes before I finally got out of the car and knocked on her door. The saltines were not helping. I was sicker than usual today, especially after I got up. What if I could not make it through my shift? I had told Adam I'd stick around the rest of the week, then I was taking a few months off. I had two more shifts to go. I just needed to make it through until then.

I almost made it to the door when I had to bend over and vomit in the bushes.

The door opened, and Troy ran to my side.

"Olivia, are you okay? Do you have the flu?"

I shook my head.

"Come in, have a glass of water."

I pursed my lips together, worried he'd smell my vomit, and made my way to the couch.

He brought me a glass of filtered water and I took a few sips, then reached into my purse for a piece of gum. He sat down next to me while I hunched over and held my head in my hands.

"I'm okay, really. Thank you for the water. I'm here to pick up Lizzy."

"She's not here," he said. "I thought maybe she stayed with you last night."

I shook my head. Where the hell could she be? "Are you sure?"

"I just checked her room."

I called her on my phone and reached her voicemail.

"I bet she was exhausted and stayed at one of the nurse's houses in Virginia last night," Troy said.

I nodded. "I bet she did. It's just weird she didn't text me. She did a double last night."

My phone beeped with an incoming text from Lizzy.

Lizzy: Stayed in Virginia last night. Long night. Sorry for the late notice. See you at work.

I tried to shake away my concern. She was okay. That's all that mattered. "You were right. She stayed in Virginia."

He smiled at me, and I forgot about my upset stomach.

"I have to go to work." I stood up and fell backward onto the couch.

He clasped my arm. "You aren't going anywhere until you have something to eat. You probably shouldn't go to work. I think you have the flu."

"Do you have any saltines?"

He ran into the kitchen and came back with crackers. "Will these work?"

I popped one in my mouth and chewed slowly, afraid to eat too fast and get sick again.

"Why don't you call in sick and lie down, okay? You need to take care of yourself."

I was pretty sure I could not move if I tried.

I sent Adam a text, then Lizzy, before I turned my ringer off. I thought I was hallucinating when Troy came back with a blanket and covered me up. I could not move or open my eyes. Everything hurt, and I was weak. I needed sleep and I could not fight it anymore.

I woke up close to noon and checked my phone. I sat up to take a drink of the water on the end table. When I lifted it to my mouth, I saw the note: I'm working at the store if you want to say hello. I have amazing muffins and coffee or tea if your stomach can tolerate it. Hope you're feeling better.

I stood up and felt so much better. I made my way to the coffee shop and saw him up on a ladder, changing a sign. The bell on the door caught his attention, and he looked my way. "Good morning, Sleeping Beauty. How are you feeling?"

He walked down the ladder and placed it to the side.

"Much better. Thank you for taking care of me."

"I can leave work early and give you a ride to Urgent Care, if you want."

I shook my head. "I'm okay. I don't think they can do anything for me."

"Coffee?" he said, holding up a coffee cup.

"Do you have any ginger tea?"

"Sure do."

I sat down at the counter while he made my tea.

"Can I have one of these, too?" I said, pointing at the cinnamon roll in the plastic display.

"You sure your stomach can handle that?"

I waved him off. "I guess I'll find out, huh?"

He shook his head and handed me the tea. "Careful. It's hot."

"Is that why there's steam coming out the top?"

He smirked. "A bit sassy today."

I shrugged. "No more than usual."

"True," he said.

I got up while my tea cooled and made my way to the romance section. "I love books."

"Me too."

"I'd assumed as much because you have a bookstore."

"The store was my wife's idea."

He cleared his throat and turned away. He still struggled to talk about Victoria.

"Tell me about her," I said, picking up the newest Viola Shipman book and flipping through it. My eyes met his.

"She was my person. She got sick, and I thought she was in remission. When she found out she wasn't going to make it, she hid it from all of her friends, family, and me."

"Why?"

He shrugged. "I guess she wanted everyone to treat her normal. When she had cancer, she felt like we were all so worried about her all the time and she just wanted to live what was left of her life to the fullest. She refused any more treatments."

I brought the book over to the counter and sat down. "That must have been really hard for you."

"It was."

"How long did she hide it?"

He smiled and laughed. "Too long. She actually made me a dating profile and tried to set me up before she was gone."

"No way!"

"I'm not kidding." The muscles in his jaw tightened. His strong jawline was so attractive. I caught myself staring and returned my eyes to my tea. "She tried to set you up while she was still alive?"

"She was selfless like that."

"Most people search their whole life for a soulmate like that. You're really lucky, you know."

"Not lucky enough." He shook his head. "Sometimes I wish I would have gone first. Here she was being selfless, and I wished it were me instead of her. Selfish, I know."

"How is that selfish?"

He had to be the kindest man I'd ever met, and his love was so deep. Although I was attracted to him, I was not at all jealous. Victoria must have been perfect, like he was.

"Because she'd be the one left alone, grieving."

"I don't think that's selfish. I think it's sweet. Really sweet."

He grabbed a rag and cleaned the counter to calm down. He loved her so much my heart hurt for him.

"Lizzy told me I should move on and try to be happy, but I'm not ready. It feels like it was just yesterday."

I said nothing. I don't think he needed me to. Instead, I listened.

"I know Victoria told Lizzy to help me move on, but I never will."

"Never?"

He was too young to decide to stay single forever. He deserved happiness.

"I don't know. I won't ever get over her."

"I don't think anyone expects you to get over Victoria. They just want you to be happy. No one will ever take her place, you know. Whatever you decide, just make sure you follow your heart."

He put his hands on the counter to steady himself.

"Well, I should probably get going. Tim is going to wonder where I went."

He nodded, sadness in his eyes. "Thank you for listening, Olivia."

I put my hand on his cheek before turning around.

"I struggle to talk about her, you know. Like this anyway. But I trust you and feel comfortable talking to you. Thank you. Really."

"Always."

Chapter 25

Lizzy

I didn't remember falling asleep, but I woke up with my head in Adam's lap. A strange way to wake up.

"Good morning," he whispered, running his fingers through my hair and tucking it behind my ear.

I rubbed my eyes and sat up.

Last night flashed through my mind. It was hard wrap my mind around what happened yesterday. To be punched by a doctor while doing my job was so tough for me to process.

I struggled to catch my breath. "Can I jump in your shower quick? I need to wake up before I go to work."

"Maybe you need to take the day off. Let me deal with all of this. I'm meeting with administration this morning, and Dr. Evans will no longer be a doctor by the time I'm done with him."

He was fighting for me. "Thank you. I want to go to work though. I can't afford to miss a shift and the longer I wait to go back, the harder it will be."

He put his head in his hands. "Are you sure? Is there anything I can do? Do you want me to keep him off the maternity floor today? I'll make sure he doesn't go anywhere near you."

I squeezed his arm. "I appreciate it, Adam, I really do. But I want everything to go back to normal."

I avoided telling him what Lucy said to me or I knew it would set him off. How could she question me on whether I was sure he hit me? Was this somehow my fault? Did I do something that set him off? Was there something I should have done differently? No. This was how I was trained.

"I need you to do something, though," Adam said.

I looked at him curiously. "What's that?"

"Can you take a picture of your back where he hit you and send it to me?"

I nodded. "Yeah. I can do that."

"Will you be okay if I go in right now? I want to get started on this right away. Before he hurts anyone else."

"I'll be fine."

"You sure?"

I glanced at him and forced a smile. "I'm sure."

"And if you change your mind about coming in, just let me know. Promise?" His voice was soft and protective.

I nodded. "I promise."

I took multiple pictures of my back where Dr. Evans hit me. The incident kept replaying in my mind. I called and made an appointment with my primary doctor to get it looked at. Nothing was showing up in the picture, but it sure hurt to the touch.

I took a deep breath and walked into the hospital. I kept looking over my shoulder to see if anyone was staring at me. Did everyone know? Did they think it was my fault?

I put on my blinders when I walked onto the maternity floor. I did not look anyone in the eyes. I was here to do my job, and that would be a tremendous accomplishment today.

We had two mothers in labor and no Dr. Evans in sight. Neither of the expectant mothers had Dr. Evans as their doctor, so I was relieved. I made my way to chart at the nursing station. Lucy was eyeing me up from behind the desk.

"Good morning," I said, not looking her directly in the eyes. We had shift change handoff where we reported what was going on with our patients to the next shift of nurses, but I never even looked at Lucy or Tanya when they spoke. I was here to work, then go home. I wanted to disappear into a room and forget all about yesterday.

My body was stiff and the stress and worry was getting to me.

Adam stepped out of his office. "Lizzy, when you get a chance, will you come into my office?"

Lucy shook her head my way and made eye contact before rolling her eyes.

I walked past her, and she grabbed my arm gently. "Don't make this a bigger deal than it already is," she said with warning in her voice. "Don't do this to Peggy. It'll embarrass her."

I pulled my arm out of her grasp and did not give her another second of my time. Sides were already being drawn, but what had I done wrong?

Peggy was Dr. Evans' wife. She was a nurse on our floor. She knew her husband was a jerk, but never said anything. I always secretly believed he was abusive toward her. She seemed to run in the opposite direction when he was around.

Once in his office, Adam closed the door. "Did you take that picture for me?"

I shook my head. "Not yet," I lied. I was embarrassed to send the picture to him. There was no bruise. The spot was so light it looked like nothing.

"I spoke to administration and they want a picture by the end of the day. Please, send it to me tonight, okay?"

I hadn't decided whether I would send a photo to him or not. I had an appointment the next morning with my doctor and I wanted to wait and see what he had to say first. My doctor's office was in Hibbing, so I did not think there was a conflict of interest. He knew Doctor Evans, but I had a feeling he was not a fan, either. Few people were.

"What did the administration say?"

"They're going to look into it and get back to me. I told them he admitted it to you and apologized, which is good. It tells them he isn't in denial. He needs to lose his license. Maybe they will convince him to take an early retirement." He stared into my eyes and squeezed my arm. "I won't let this go, Lizzy. As of right now, he isn't allowed on this floor because they have opened up a formal investigation."

I suddenly felt nauseated and had to sit down. "What does that mean? Is everyone going to know?"

He raised his voice. "Lizzy, you're the victim here. Don't let his actions make you feel like the guilty one. He made this choice. He hit you. Doctors can't go around assaulting nurses without repercussions. It's not okay."

He was right, but I just wanted this all to go away. If I was the victim, why did I feel like this was my fault?

As the day went on, I kept my head down and did my job. It helped to know Dr. Evans wouldn't show up on our floor. I did not need to be afraid.

A woman in labor was wheeled up to our floor when I

was almost done with my shift. Lucy asked her who her doctor was and when she said Dr. Evans, Lucy's eyes burned right through me.

"I'm sorry, he isn't available," Lucy said.

"What? But I'm in labor. He never said anything about being gone. He promised he'd be here. Who will deliver my baby? He's delivered my other two kids. Why? Why isn't he here?"

She was in panic mode. Her body was in pain, and her hormones were getting the best of her. Instead of calming her down, Lucy looked at me and said, "Lizzy, do you want to explain why her doctor isn't here?"

I turned around and walked out that door and to the nurses' station. I was so angry I did not say a word through shift change. I got the hell out of there as quick as I could, and I did not shed a tear. I had three days off and I never wanted to go back, not ever again.

Chapter 26

Olivia

I called Lizzy three times, but she did not pick up her phone. She had to be home by now. Did she pick up another double shift? I put my shoes on and made my way over to Troy's house to check on her. Troy was planting flowers in the flowerbed in front of his house.

He turned to look at me. "Hey there, Ima. How are you feeling?"

"Much better. I have been trying to reach Lizzy, but she isn't answering her phone. Is she home yet?"

"Yeah, she got home a bit ago. She said she was exhausted and not feeling well and was going to bed. She said she didn't want to be bothered by anyone." He got up and took off his gardening gloves. "To be honest, she seemed really upset. You two work together. Did something happen at work?"

"Not that I know of."

"I'm sure it's nothing, then." He looked around. "It's a beautiful night. Want to go for a walk?"

I had nothing better to do, and I'd been lying around all

day. I needed to get my butt moving. Not getting any exercise could not be good for the baby. "Sure, why not?"

We made our way down Turtle Creek Road and onto Greenrock Road, then West Sturgeon Forrest Road. Troy said the view was beautiful, and I really needed a nature view to lift my spirits. "No bears?"

He laughed at that.

Hope followed along, nipping at my heels.

The wind was light, and the sun was still warm and bright. "I love this time of year because the sun doesn't set until nine o'clock."

"Yeah, much better than a six o'clock sunset in the winter, right?"

The smell of pine trees and freshly cut grass filled my senses. The humidity was heavy in the air, and it reminded me of some of the best days of my summers as a child. "I never thought I'd like a place as much as I loved living in Duluth with the perfect view of Lake Superior out of my bedroom window, but Side Lake is definitely in competition."

"Oh, really."

"Yeah. It's so peaceful here. And beautiful."

The crickets and frogs chirped louder, as if on cue. "This town is really growing on me."

"Just wait until this weekend. The Fourth of July may be the busiest day of the year, but it is also the best. No one does the fourth like Side Lake."

"Is that so?"

His strong jawline was prevalent from this angle. I wanted to touch it. I wanted to hold his face. Why was this force so strong? He was a widower, and I was a pregnant woman with far too many hormones. I had to pull myself together.

A dizzy spell passed over me and I stopped mid step and crouched. I had not eaten anything for a while.

Troy stopped beside me. "Are you okay?"

"Just give me a minute. I'm a little lightheaded."

He crouched down next to me. "Are you sure you're okay? I still think you have the flu."

I shook my head.

"Are you diabetic?"

I shook my head again.

"Are you sure?"

"Troy, I'm pregnant, okay?"

He deadpanned. After an uncomfortable silence, he cleared his throat and stood up. He put his hands on his hips and looked away from me. "Why didn't you tell me?"

Of course, this was all about him. What did it matter? "I haven't told many people. I'm still trying to figure this all out myself."

He turned toward me and sat down on the road. "I'm sorry. That was rude. I didn't mean that. I'm just in shock, that's all."

I nodded. He was disappointed in me. Maybe he felt betrayed. I could not be sure what was going on in his head. I dropped to my butt next to him.

"Does your ex know?" he said.

I nodded, but I could not get any words out.

"And he's not on board?"

"Not exactly, but it doesn't matter. I want this baby. I'm happy."

He put his hand on my leg. "Then I'm happy for you."

His words were genuine. This man surprised me every time I saw him. I put my head on his shoulder.

He read my mind. "You're scared?"

"Terrified. But so happy. Did you and Victoria ever talk about having kids?"

For some reason, I was not worried about asking him. Our conversations often led to deep questions, questions most people would avoid or walk away from. Maybe even get offended by someone they just met asking them. But not with Troy. He was different. Calm, cool, and collected. I loved listening to the way he spoke, the way his words were filled with so much heart.

He stared off at the lake. "We spent most of our time together traveling until she found out she was sick. To be honest, I never thought we would have kids." He paused and for a minute, I thought he might not continue. "Then she got sick and then better, or so I thought. Not long after she told me she was terminal and done fighting that she confessed she was broken she'd never be a mother. Then she brought home Hope."

I lifted my head to look at him. "So Hope was your baby?" I stroked the back of Hope's head.

"She bought Hope because she did not want me to be alone. She knew I needed someone."

I pursed my lips and sighed. "That is the most beautiful thing I've ever heard."

Troy patted Hope on the back.

"Did it help? Did she make you feel less lonely?"

"Yes. She really did. I can't imagine life without Hope now. We've been through a lot together." He rubbed Hope under the chin and their eyes met. Hope licked his face. "Haven't we, girl?"

She barked, sounding more like a squeal. She was talking to him. I had no doubt she understood every word he said. "I never realized how beautiful nature could be. How stress relieving it could be."

He smiled.

"I told my supervisor I needed some time off until I have the baby."

"That's great. You need to listen to your body."

I never stopped to listen to my body. I had lived in a big city where work was my life because I did not want to go home. I never took a minute to think. I was either working or on my phone, and just trying to get through every day. Side Lake was a wake-up call. My divorce helped me to breathe again.

"I suppose we should get back, or Lizzy will be worried about you."

He stood up and pulled me to my feet. I wiped the rocks and sand off my butt. "I was wrong about you, Troy."

He looked confused. "What do you mean?"

"The day I met you. I had low expectations, but you proved me wrong."

"You're welcome, I guess. Wait, is this about my shooting? I really need to show you I am better than that."

I laughed. "Sure you are. Keep telling yourself that."

"I'd throw you in that lake, but that tiny human in your belly is saving you."

"I'm shaking in my boots."

His dimple popped. "You should be."

Chapter 27

Lizzy

Troy was gone when I got home, so I went straight into the shower and then to my room. I left a note on the counter to let him know I was exhausted and needed some sleep. The truth was, I did not want to talk to Troy. I wasn't ready. I wasn't ready to talk to Olivia or anyone, really. I was broken and defeated.

Adam texted me three times about a picture before I finally turned my phone off. I turned off my light and grabbed my reading light. I picked up *Lies and Weddings* from my end table to distract my thoughts. Before I knew it, I was one hundred pages into the story. Kevin Kwan's writing took me to a faraway place, but the night was late. I drifted off to sleep rather quickly, but woke up a few hours later in a sweat, sobbing.

Would this nightmare ever be over?

It took me over an hour to fall back to sleep, but this time I passed out until my alarm went off.

I tip-toed my way to the kitchen and made myself a cup of green tea and walked out onto the deck in my bathrobe. The morning was cool outside, but not cold. I stared at the beauty of the lake. The sun was rising from behind the trees, illuminating a pink and orange glow in the sky. The birds were chirping in the distance and I closed my eyes to imagine what birds they were. I had no clue. The scene looked so perfect, more like a painting in a museum. I wished I knew how to paint so I could hang a giant canvas of this scenery on my wall. I grabbed my phone and took a picture. I did not want this peaceful moment to end.

I made my way to the end of the dock and sat down with my tea. I took off my sandals and dipped my toes in the refreshing water. Against my better judgement, I looked at my phone. I had six texts from Adam and five missed calls.

Adam: I need you to call me right away.

Adam: Please.

Adam: It's important.

Adam: Maybe you went to bed. I'm coming over in the morning. We need to talk.

Adam: Okay, I don't know where you live, so call me first thing in the morning. I'll leave my ringer on. Please, Lizzy.

I was in my special place. I didn't want to ruin it by thinking about what happened, but I had no choice. He would not stop until I called him, and I knew he was just trying to be helpful. I'd call him and tell him he needs to give me a few days to think. I needed some time.

"Hello?"

His voice was a bit groggy, but he sounded anxious at the same time. "Lizzy?"

"Hey, Adam. What's going on?"

"I talked to administration. They're going to call you today, but I need to tell you something. I'll understand if you don't want to talk to me again. I'm so sorry, Lizzy. I screwed up big time."

He was in panic mode, but I did not understand why. What was I missing? "Slow down, Adam. What are you talking about?"

"You know how I kept asking you to send me a picture?"

"Yeah."

"Well, you didn't, and I panicked and I sent them a picture of you."

I could not breathe. What was he talking about? He had pictures of me? "I'm confused. What are you talking about?"

The phone went silent. Nothing was adding up.

"I couldn't keep working there if Dr. Evans was still there. I did it for you, Lizzy. I did it for you."

He was rambling. What was he even saying?

"Adam, are you okay?"

"No. I had my sister come over and she let me hit her and I sent the picture to administration and told them it was you. I'm sending you the picture now. Please don't be mad. I couldn't let him stay there. I had to, Lizzy. I don't care if I lose my job or my license. It isn't right. He could hurt someone else. I know I went about this the wrong way and I'm sorry. I was desperate. There was no other way."

I could still hear his ramblings as I pulled the phone away from my ear and checked his message. The picture was of a woman's right shoulder with a bruise. It looked like she was hit multiple times.

"Adam, what is this? What did you do? Please tell me you didn't send this to them."

"I'm sorry." He sounded as if he was a foot away from his phone.

"I wanted to prepare you. They're going to call you. It looks like your shoulder. Please, I know it sounds terrible, but please just think about it."

"Think about what?" I no longer recognized my own voice. I was angry, pissed off. I felt betrayed. "How could you, Adam? I don't understand."

"Please don't hate me. I did it for you. He needs to lose his license."

I groaned loud, no longer able to control my frustration. I spoke through clenched teeth. "I can't talk to you right now. Adam, I feel like I don't know you. How could you? What the hell? I need to go before I say something I don't mean."

"No, please. Talk to me," he pleaded. "I'm sorry. I'm so sorry. I had to do this."

"I'm turning off my phone for a few days. Please, just let me think, okay."

"That's all I'm asking," he said, pleading. "They will never know."

"But I'll know!"

How dare he take this away from me? How dare he put this on me. I would be a fraud. How could I live with myself?

"I'm sorry."

That was the last word I heard before I hung up my

phone and threw it in the lake. I curled into a ball right there on the dock and cried so hard my eyes swelled up. I was no longer the victim. He took that away from me. I was just as bad as that asshole of a doctor. How could I ever go back there now? How could I face everyone?

"Help me, Aunt Victoria. Tell me what to do. I don't know what to do anymore," I whispered into the wind.

A part of me expected a bird to fly by or a loon to splash in the water to show me she was there with me. She was listening. Instead, all I heard was the loud beating of my heart in my chest. I closed my eyes. Life had to be better than this.

Chapter 28

Olivia

I followed Troy back to his house so I could talk to Lizzy. We walked through the kitchen and found a note on the counter. He picked it up and I read it over his shoulder.

Lizzy was not feeling well. That made two of us, but I was starting to wonder if something happened to her. It was not like Lizzy to not text me or check in. We'd gotten so close.

I met up with everyone the night before the Fourth of July to work on the float at Kat and Ethan's house. The float was almost finished and sitting on a trailer. Us women were dressing up like mermaids and the guys like Turtles, except Ethan. Ethan would be King Triton. He did not like to be the center of attention, but Kat talked him into it.

My baby bump was more noticeable now, so I decided to tell everyone on the Fourth of July when they all had a few drinks in them. There was no reason to hide it from them. They were my friends now, too.

Maddy's eyes lit up when she saw me. "Olivia, I'm so glad you're here. We were worried about you. Tim said you have been working a lot. Do you like your new job?"

"I actually had to take leave."

Everyone looked at me with concern.

Troy gave me an encouraging smile and stepped to my side. This was my opportunity. "I'm pregnant."

Everyone congratulated me and I got hugs all around.

Troy was last, and he leaned in and whispered, "I'm so damn proud of you. You're going to be a great mom."

I broke out in goosebumps from his words, and a smile that would not go away lit up my face. It felt so good to finally tell everyone.

Lizzy had been quiet the last few days, and I worried she was upset about my sudden departure from the hospital. I'd let her down, and she was ghosting me. Troy said she was in bed with another headache. This time, I was not taking that as an excuse. As soon as we finished with the float, I made my way to Troy's house and knocked.

"Lizzy, it's me. I'm coming in."

I opened the door and there she lay, curled into a ball, sobbing.

I hurried to her bed and cradled her head in my lap. "What's going on? Are you okay? Oh, sweetie."

Why didn't I come sooner? Why did I let it go this long without making sure she was okay?

"It's bad, Liv. It's terrible."

"What's bad?" She told me everything, and I stared at her in shock. She was now sitting cross-legged on the bed, her eyes swollen.

"I can't believe he hit you. He was bad, but you have to be kidding me. I know it isn't what you want to hear, but I get why Adam did what he did."

She glared at me.

I put out my hand. "Not that I think it's okay. I don't."

She looked down and picked at her comforter. "What do I do?"

"You need to call administration."

She shook her head. "And say what? I am so scared to talk to them. My phone is at the bottom of a lake. It's a long story. I called in for a few extra days using Troy's phone. I'm scared, Liv, I'm so scared."

I wanted to make her feel better. Give her some encouraging words that would help her, but she was right. She was screwed. Adam lied, and it would come out soon enough.

"What do you think is the right thing to do?"

She knew the answer, even if she did not want to do it. The answer needed to be her idea. "What do you think?"

"I need to call administration and tell them it wasn't my picture."

"You absolutely do. What did the doctor say about your bruise? Did you have a bruise?"

She nodded and stood up to grab a piece of paper off her dresser.

I read it. "Physical Finding: Contusion on the right scapula and rhomboid. Diagnosis: Acute Contusion of right shoulder." I stared at the words before me. "You have a case here."

"I'm scared," she said. "I'm so scared."

She leaned into my shoulder, and I wrapped my arms around her. "I know. I'll be right there with you. Call administration. It's the right thing to do. You aren't the one who told them the picture was of you, Adam was."

She nodded, still distraught.

I handed her my phone, and she made the call.

She got off the phone and took a deep breath.

"How do you feel?"

"A little better."

"How about we go for a walk down to the dock? It's busy down there with boats and jet skis for the Fourth, but I think it'll be good for you to take in some summer air.

"I'd like that."

"Oh, and by the way, I might have accidentally told everyone I was pregnant."

"It's about time," she said with a smile.

Chapter 29

Lizzy

I snoozed my alarm twice before I finally got up and hopped in the shower. Maddy made Kat's and my costumes by hand for the float. Kat was Ariel, so she could stand by King Triton, and I was one of her sisters. Maddy ended up surprising us with The Little Mermaid costumes instead of turtles because she said the turtles were just too boring and we needed to win. Kevin was Sebastian and Brad was Scuttle. Troy was Prince Eric with a big Elvis-looking wig, for which he got a lot of crap from the guys. Tim was a shark, and Josh was the chef. The rest of us were Ariel's sisters. I had shells on my chest made of felt and a giant tail that we snapped on. We sat on the float because we would trip and fall if we had to walk.

Tim sat next to me on the teal crepe paper. Ariel and King Triton sat inside a giant purple clam shell. Emma was dressed up as Ursula. Her tentacles were brilliant and dragged stiffly while she walked. Little David and Brittany were dressed as Ursula's eels and handed out candy to the kids. Everyone on the float had squirt guns that we shot at all the innocent bystanders, who opened up their arms.

The weather was hot and humid, normal for Minnesota in early July. Sweat was dripping down my back and I wet my feet a few times to cool down. At one point, Josh was chasing Kevin around with a fake sword that lit up, the chef chasing the crab. Everyone broke out in laughter, including me.

We were by far the best float in the parade. Troy would hop off the float and hand out bookmarks and coupons to his store. Everyone roared. I was not sure if it was our costumes or the famous author on the float that drew the cheers from the crowd. The moment was magical, and Ethan was so humble. Some of the crowd walked right up to the float just to shake his hand.

Troy handed out pink ribbons with a big smile. It felt like Aunt Victoria was there with us.

I was having the most miserable week of my life and here I was, smiling from ear to ear without a worry in the world. I decided at that moment I would leave the stress behind and focus on a wonderful weekend with my friends and family, celebrating Independence Day and having the time of my life. Side Lake was right where I needed to be.

The streets were packed, and the judges were waiting on the side once we reached the last two blocks of the parade. We all posed for a picture and waved at the camera. We acted like we were surprised when we took first place, but we all knew we would. We not only had the best float, but the best time out there.

Olivia, Troy, Tim, Kat, Ethan and I all made our way down to Riverside while the rest of our friends went to Bimbos for the kids' party. The sun was warm and my shirt was sticking to me. The parking lot was full. Tables outside the restaurant were set up to sell bracelets for entrance to the back-yard where a band was playing and a bocce ball tournament was ongoing.

Tim and I teamed up for the bocce ball tournament, at my insistence, along with Troy and Olivia. Kat and Ethan got in on the bean bag tournament. Tim was as good as I expected him to be and he carried our team. I was not terrible, and a few times I hit the white ball away from our opponents' red one. We ended up taking second, but Troy and Olivia were eliminated quite early, and I had not seen them in an hour.

After we received our $150 in prize money, we went inside to celebrate and get some food. The tables were all full, and the restaurant was crowded upstairs. We found a place at the bar and slid in before anyone else had a chance.

Riverside was known for their Colorado Bulldogs, and Tim and I both ordered our second one of the day. They made them strong enough to burn your esophagus going down. My favorite part about the bulldogs was the hazel-nuts on the top.

"Wow, that's strong," Tim said with a grimace.

"Who is that, over there in the blue hat?"

He turned his head to look, and I grabbed one of his hazelnuts and put it in my mouth. He did not notice.

"Who?"

I pointed behind him. "By the bathroom in the blue hat."

He turned again, and I grabbed another one off the top of his drink. When I went back for the last and final hazel-nut, he caught me and the nut slipped out of my finger and popped up on the top of his drink again.

"Hey!" he said and covered his drink with his hand. He swatted my hand away. "How will I ever trust you again?"

I shrugged and reached for the hazelnut. This time, he let me grab it without a fight.

"I don't like them, anyway. They're all yours."

My leg bumped his, and I felt my face grow warm.

"Tell me about nursing school. Was it fun? Did you meet a lot of new friends? Was it exhausting?"

I took a swig of my bulldog. "Extremely hard, but I met a few people I bonded with, and we had a lot of study sessions at Caribou. The first year was more book work and memorization, then the second year was all hands on. I loved it, even if it was exhausting."

He leaned in closer, and his eyes stared into mine. "I never really got to tell you, but I'm very proud of you."

"Thanks."

He paused and stared at me as if he wanted to say something, but he hesitated. "Is everything okay?"

I looked away. "What do you mean?"

He tucked my hair behind my ear. "You haven't seemed like yourself lately."

I stirred the straw in my glass. "Just some stuff going on at work has been really difficult." Me and my big mouth. I did not want to talk about it but I always felt so comfortable talking to him.

"You don't like your new position? I thought this was what you wanted."

I nodded. "No, it is. I just—"

"Tim—I was hoping to find you here. I saw the two of you took second place in the bocce tourney. Great job."

Tim stood up and shook hands with a good-looking guy with a perfect smile. The hand shake turned into a hug with a hard slap on the back.

Tim put his arm around me. "Lizzy, this is Dawson.

Dawson is a teacher at Bob Dylan Elementary. I haven't seen you in what...a year now?"

"Yeah, it's been a while." He put his arm around the stunning woman next to him. "You know my wife, Emily."

The beautiful, petite blonde smiled politely.

The band and all the people talking were so loud we had to shout just to hear one another.

"Anyway, we're meeting some friends over at Bimbos," Dawson said. "The kids are having a blast, but we had to sneak away and check out the Riv. It was great to see you, man. Don't be a stranger. You know where we live, right?"

"Absolutely," Tim said, shaking Dawson's hand again. He leaned in to hug Emily.

"Do you know everyone in this town?" I said in a playful tone. "You've only been here a few years now, but you seem to know everyone."

Was I flirting with him? The alcohol made me feel like I didn't care. What was the harm?

"Want to walk to Josh and Whitney's house now?"

I leaned in to talk in his ear so he could hear me over the loud voices around us. "Aren't they still at Bimbos'?"

"Yeah, but everyone is meeting there in an hour, so we can take the boat out to McCarthy's to listen to the band. It's just so loud in here."

"Sure, why not?"

I drank the rest of my drink through the straw so it would be gone faster, and Tim did the same.

We walked out the door and headed down the road, watching the traffic as they drove by. There were four wheelers and bicyclers. The sides of the road were packed with people. The weather was perfect to spend the Fourth at the lake and everyone was taking advantage of it.

"It's crazy to see all the people out here. Usually it's steady with people, but nothing like this," Tim said.

We walked past the Side Lake Store and Tim looked at me with a nod. "Ice cream?"

We walked up and saw a family sat outside on the bench eating ice cream. There were people all over the parking lot eating their cones. "I'm not sure how well ice cream will mix with the liquor, but why not? Hopefully, they have cake batter. That's my absolute favorite," I said.

A few people stood in line, but it did not take long before we got our cones. Tim chose the same flavor as I did and paid.

"Thank you," I said, a mouth full of ice cream.

"Come look," he said, leading me down the aisle. "They have Side Lake key chains and stickers. I want this shirt." He pointed to a T-shirt with 'Life is better in Side Lake' written on it.

I picked up a blue onesie. "I want to get this for Olivia's baby. Isn't it the cutest?"

He held it up against his chest. "Yes, it's going to be a Side Lake baby. She'll love it."

We made our way around the store.

"For a gas station, it sure has a lot of useful stuff."

"The owners love to support local small businesses and they like to carry what the people around the lake may need so they don't have to run all the way into town for it."

"That makes sense."

Once we paid and continued our walk, we both struggled to talk because the humidity had the ice cream melting faster than we could eat it. My hand was all sticky, and I looked over at Tim, who dropped a big glob on his pants. Right by his zipper.

I had a napkin in my hand and dropped to my knees to clean it up without even thinking about it.

I heard him snort before I even wiped it away and I realized what this must look like.

"Oh, quit being a guy," I said with a laugh.

Someone behind us whistled, and then we heard laughter. I threw the napkin at him and stood up. "I guess this wasn't the best idea."

We both started laughing.

"I'm sorry, but it was funny, you have to admit."

I took a bite of my cone and the ice cream dropped right on my chest.

His eyes widened, and he reached toward me with the napkin.

"Don't even think about it."

I grabbed the napkin and started dabbing at the splotch.

Tim wiped his ice cream on my face.

"You didn't!"

He started running, and I chased him. He dropped his cone on the ground, but I did not slow down until I was laughing so hard I wet my pants. Not a complete bladder leak, but enough to leave a dark wet stain.

He immediately took off his T-shirt and put it in my hand.

"Here, hold this over it. We're almost at Whitney and Josh's house."

I crossed my legs and bent over with laughter, holding the T-shirt in front of my pants. "I can't believe that just happened. Oh. My. Gosh. Olivia and Kat aren't going to believe this. This is a day I'm never going to forget."

I probably should have been embarrassed, but I just laughed.

Chapter 30

Olivia

We were both terrible at Bocce ball and we forfeited our first game.

"I should probably run back to the house and let Hope out. Want to go for a ride?" Troy said.

"Absolutely."

At Troy's house, we opened the door and Hope came jumping up on me and licked my face.

"Hope, down!" Troy said sternly.

"It's fine. She's so cute."

"You sure?"

"Yeah, I'm sure."

We were outside, standing by his store.

"I love your apple tree. It looks so healthy."

"It's still pretty small. I don't get many apples off it yet. I planted it at the grand opening of my store as a tribute to Victoria. We did a ceremony and sprinkled her ashes."

"That's beautiful," I said.

"I think she would have wanted that."

He wiped the sweat from his forehead with his shirt. "Sure is hot out. Want to jump in the lake with me?"

"You don't need to ask me twice." I peeled off my tank top and revealed my pink bikini top. We walked down the steps and I took off my shoes and shorts. When I looked at him, he was staring at my belly.

I was showing just enough.

I turned around and ran down the dock and jumped in. He was right behind me. He dove in and came up smiling as he shook his hair, the water hitting me in the face.

"So that's where Hope gets it. Or did you learn how to do that from her?"

He laughed and splashed me. I tried to get away, but he swam after me and grabbed me around the waist. But he quickly let go.

"You won't hurt the baby. You didn't grab me that hard."

He looked relieved.

I splashed him this time and then jumped on his back. He wrapped my legs around his torso and I held onto his arms. His shoulders were ripped, and the shape of his back was like an hourglass. I wrapped my arms around his neck and put my chin on his shoulder. He did the breast stroke with me on his back. I relaxed and enjoyed the feeling of his body beneath me.

He stood up, and I slipped off his back. He pulled me to him, our stomachs touching. He looked down at my stomach again with tenderness in his eyes.

"How does it feel having another person inside you?"

"It's unbelievable. To be responsible for another human inside me. This baby has already changed my life and my thinking. I would fight the world for him or her, you know?"

The water was up to the top of my thighs. He put his hand out.

"Can I?"

I nodded, and he touched my belly. I held my hand over his.

"Unbelievable," he whispered.

We both leaned in, this time without hesitation. Our lips touched. My body warmed. His lips were perfect.

My arms wrapped around his neck, deepening my hold on him and our kiss. His hands wrapped tighter around my body. He lifted me and I wrapped my legs around him. Our lips pulled away for a second and we both looked into each other's eyes before diving right back into the best kiss of my life.

The heaviness in my chest, the worry, it was all gone. I bit his lip as we pulled away, and he laughed, kissing me again.

"You are so damn beautiful, Ima. You know that?"

I smiled and shook my head. I was never good with taking compliments.

"From the moment I met you, I knew you would be trouble. I was scared of the powerful feelings I had for you, but everything about you feels so right."

He set my legs back in the water and we walked out of the lake, side-by-side, holding hands.

He turned to me just before we got to the dock and lifted me off the ground and spun me in a circle.

"I never want this moment to end."

We made our way to McCarthy's to listen to the band, and we ate a picnic lunch on the boat. The kids were busy going up and down the slide. The rest of us were tanning on the boat or splashing around in the water.

After lunch, we cruised around the lakes in the pontoon and pulled the kids behind in a tube. By the end of the day, we were exhausted and sunburnt and ready to relax. Kat and Ethan had made pizza dough. We all made our own wood fire pizzas and cooked them ourselves in their new stove. The guests from their B&B hung out with us until we made our way back to McCarthy's beach to watch the fireworks.

We parked the boat on the shore and sat in the sand to watch the show high in the sky. Tim pulled out the bug spray once the mosquitoes found us, and I lay back in the sand as the bright colors lit up the sky. Troy was laying next to me, his hand lightly brushing mine.

I tried not to think about it too much. I just wanted to enjoy the moment as our kisses replayed in my mind.

Once the fireworks were over, Troy helped me into the boat. He sat down next to me and put a blanket on my lap. He rubbed my shoulders, not caring who could see. His actions surprised our friends, I'm sure, but no one made a big deal about it. I relaxed into his shoulder, and he wrapped his arms around me.

I glanced at Tim and Lizzy. They looked like they were getting cozy, too. This was a Fourth of July I would not forget.

Chapter 31

Lizzy

We woke up early the next morning and headed to Bimbo's for the Firecracker 5k. Everyone was running or walking it in our group. Brittany and David were even on board. Residents and summer people lined the sides of the road. They handed out water and cheered us on.

The first stretch of the race was hot, but when we ran into the shadows of the trees, bugs attacked and overwhelmed us.

I rounded a corner, and that's when I saw the hill going straight up. Running up that hill would pull a muscle. I had no choice but to walk.

Olivia panted next to me. "It's so hot. This is such a challenging course."

The last turn was onto highway five. It took everything I had to keep running. Olivia encouraged me to go ahead while she walked. She was worried about getting dehydrated, and I agreed. I reached the bottom of the hill and the finish line. Tim jumped out from the side of the road and ran with me.

"You are killing it. Push through, you got this."

He stopped and went back to the side of the road. Everyone cheered loudly as I finished at thirty-two minutes flat. I was proud of my time. If only I had practiced. Maybe next year I could beat that time. I smiled and waved at the crowd.

Tim ran up the sideline to meet me at the finish line with a bottle of water and a granola bar just seconds after I stopped running.

"How are you feeling?"

I leaned over, my hand on my knees. "Like I'm very out of shape." I stood up, still trying to catch my breath. "But also like I want to get faster and do it again."

He laughed. "Sounds like you're a runner."

Maybe I was.

My muscles ached, and with each step I felt the pain, but I liked it. I wanted to be stronger and faster. With everything going on in my life, I knew this was a great outlet. "I think I am or I'm going to be."

We spent the rest of the day boating, skiing, and just enjoying each other and the beautiful summer day.

Monday morning, I bought a new cell phone, and I was on my way back when I saw Tim walking down the road. I pulled over. "Want a ride?"

He laughed and got in the car. "You know I was out walking for some exercise, but it's hard to say no to a beautiful woman with an invitation to get in her car."

I laughed and pulled up to his house.

"Come canoeing with me?"

I sighed. "Remember the last time we went out in the canoe?"

"Please," he said with a pouty lip.

"Fine, but you better make sure we don't tip this time."

He held my hand and guided me into the canoe. The lake was calm and warm. But the sun was hiding behind the clouds, so not a lot of boats were out.

We were just about to push off the dock when I heard someone call my name. I looked up the stairs to see Adam standing there, waving and calling my name. I looked at Tim. "I'm so sorry. I didn't know he was coming."

He looked confused. He looked at Adam, then back at me.

"I'll be right back, promise." I said.

Tim's face fell, but he pushed a smile.

I wanted to say more to him, but now wasn't the time. He must have questions about who Adam was.

Tim held my hand as I stood slowly and stepped onto the dock. He did not let go of my hand once I was safetly on the dock, so I turned back to look at him.

"Would you like me to wait for you? I'll wait as long as you need. Just say the word."

I squeezed his hand. "Wait for me. I'll be back."

"What are you doing here, Adam?"

He placed his hand on my back to guide me to the house. We sat on the deck overlooking the lake.

"I'm sorry I just showed up here like this. I found your uncle's address online, and I saw your car in the driveway here, so I stopped. I hope that's okay. I needed to talk to you and it couldn't wait. Are you mad at me? I understand if you hate me. I betrayed your trust."

"I don't hate you, Adam. I couldn't hate you."

He stared at the ground, his eyes so sad.

"The real reason I'm here is because I had to talk to you in person."

"Okay."

"I quit today."

My stomach felt queasy. Adam was no longer at the hospital? Because of me? "What? Why? Well, I think I know why, but it's still so hard to hear."

"Arbitration starts next week, and I had to come forward and tell them the truth. I didn't want you to go down with me. I know you couldn't lie to them. You aren't that kind of person."

He was right. I'd never be able to live with myself. I couldn't lie, especially not on the stand. It wasn't who I was. I had to be honest.

His eyes looked so sad. "I did, however, make a statement, and Evans is still not working at the hospital."

Thank goodness.

"I told Olivia I would protect you and that's what I did. I never wanted this to fall on you, so I made sure it won't." He squeezed my arm gently.

I didn't brush him off. "Will you lose your license?"

He looked away. This whole mess was so hard for him. "Most likely, but I'm done in the medical field. I'm going to start my own business and move down south. Unless you give me a reason I shouldn't."

What was that supposed to mean? "Adam, don't get the wrong idea. I really like you and I know what you did was to protect me, but I don't feel that way about you. Is that what this was about?"

He shook his head. "No, Lizzy. I wouldn't do that. I'd never forgive myself if I didn't tell you. I've had a crush on you for a long time now, but I was your supervisor. I couldn't do anything about it."

Olivia was right.

"I needed to know if you felt the same way."

I looked at him with a sympathetic smile. "I appreciate you standing up for me. I wish you had talked to me first, but I get it. To be honest, I don't think I'll be there for long myself. The way the other nurses have treated me is so uncomfortable. I don't feel like the victim anymore. I feel like I am the one on trial."

He reached over and rubbed his thumb over my cheek. I closed my eyes.

"I'll never forget you, Adam. You're a good guy and don't you ever forget it."

He stood up and nodded.

"Take care, Lizzy. Don't let them break you. Fight for what you believe. You're the victim. Don't you forget it."

My eyes teared up as I watched him walk away. What he did was wrong and it made me look bad, but his intentions were good. If only I felt the same way about him, but my heart was already taken, and I hated to admit it.

I made my way down the steps to the canoe, where Tim was still sitting.

He turned around and looked at me, and his entire face lit up. A part of me wondered if he thought I would return. "I'm back."

He held out his hand for me and I stepped in the canoe, a bit wobbly, but I was getting much better at this. I sat down and leaned forward, grabbing both of his hands in mine.

"That was Adam. He's my supervisor."

Now he really looked confused.

"It's not what you think. Trust me. I have so much I need to tell you, but first I want you to know I'm not ready for this to be over. I want to give us a shot, if you're still willing."

He kissed me before I had a chance to finish my speech. I kissed him back and heard whistling from the top of the hill.

Troy. I gave him the friendly finger, and he waved back with a smile.

"Let's take the canoe out. I need to tell you something."

He paddled at a steady rhythm as I told him about what happened to me, not missing a single detail. When I finished, he stopped paddling, a look of concern written all over his face. "Arbitration, huh? Why not court?"

"I guess it's pretty expensive."

"That's crap, Lizzy."

"I know."

He stared into the distance.

"What's on your mind, Tim?"

"I feel terrible that you're going through this. And your boss. How do you feel about what he did?"

I shrugged. "It doesn't matter anymore. He quit."

"Is that why he was here?"

"Yes. And he wanted to see if I had feelings for him."

He bit his lip, and I leaned forward and kissed him again.

"I'm not going to lie. I wanted to. I didn't want to admit I still loved you, but I do." I was flubbing it. "I'm not good at this, Tim."

"Me neither, but then again, I've never had anyone in my life I've wanted to keep."

"I feel the same way. But I want to take it slow."

He started paddling again. "I won't get down on one knee. Yet anyway."

I rolled my eyes and laughed.

"My timing wasn't great. I know that. I was insensitive to ask you when your aunt just died, but in my head I thought it would help you feel better."

I believed him, and I wanted him. I would not let him go this time.

Chapter 32

Olivia

"I can't believe you're having a baby! I'm so excited to be an aunty again," Maddy said.

Maddy was sitting at Tim's kitchen table where I was making homemade quiche. A week had gone by since my kiss with Troy. He was busy with the store and had not been around much.

Today was the day Lizzy had arbitration. She was sitting at the table, pushing her food around on her plate. Her phone rang.

She jumped to her feet to answer. "Hello?"

She made her way outside and shut the door. When she finally came back, she had tears in her eyes.

"Who was that?" I said.

She wiped her face and smiled. "Tonya, one of the nurses from work. She wanted to wish me luck today and let me know she was thinking of me. Most of them have really been supportive. There were only a few who wo't look at me."

"That says a lot about the kind of people they are. They

don't realize you are doing this for all of them. You are strong, Lizzy."

She took a deep breath and smiled. "Thanks, Liv."

I nodded.

Maddy gave us both hugs. "Good luck, Lizzy." She bent over and placed her hand on my stomach. "Goodbye, baby."

I laughed.

I changed into the only outfit I had that was nice and still fit me. My stomach seemed to expand overnight. I needed to make it into town to buy some new clothes.

We picked up Tim, but he and I had to wait outside the courtroom, which was in the hospital. Arbitration was just like court, but less formal and less expensive than court. I was a little nervous when Lizzy told me the decision would be binding and she was okay with whatever they decided. An actual court might be a more impartial and fairer.

I hated not being in there with Lizzy when she testified, but she assured me she would be okay. We waited outside for over an hour. We watched Dr. Evans go in. He never glanced our way, nor did he look nervous. That was what it must be like when you don't have a conscience.

After he went in, Peggy, Dr. Evans' wife, sat down next to me.

"Hi," she said.

I'd only met her once, but Lizzy had told me she was a sweet lady, and that Dr. Evans might be treating her poorly as well. How could she be here supporting him?

"You're Olivia, right?"

I nodded and tried hard not to glare at her. How dare she support him after he hit a nurse, her friend and co-worker?

Some of the other nurses treated Lizzy badly. My anxiety spiked.

"I came here to support my husband, but I don't think I can," Peggy said.

That was a shock. What exactly was she saying? I held my breath.

In a voice barely above a whisper, she said, "I told him I didn't want to be here. That I wanted to stay out of it."

Tim's eyes widened. He was as curious as I was about what she was about to say.

She rolled up her sleeve and showed us the bruises. They were yellow, blue, and purple, like she had a sleeve of tattoos. "This is what happens when I defy my husband."

Her lip quivered, and I automatically reached for her hand. She squeezed my hand back.

Tears streaked down her face. "I won't keep quiet anymore. I can't let him continue to do this to other people."

I reached into my purse and handed her a tissue.

"I'm going to testify. He needs to lose his license. Please tell Lizzy I'm sorry it took me so long."

She got up and walked to the end of the hallway to meet Kevin, who was in his uniform and vest. They walked back together. He nodded at Tim and me and opened the doors to the courtroom. The doors shut behind them. Tim and I both leaned closer to the door to hear what was going on, but we heard nothing.

Tim stood up and paced the hallway as he tried to listen. "What do you think she's doing?"

"The right thing," I said. "I think she's had enough."

Dr. Evans came out of the courtroom in handcuffs, and it took everything I had not to punch him in the face. We made eye contact, and Kevin stopped in front of me with his grip on Dr. Evan's arm.

He looked me in the eye, and I glared at him.

"I hope they lose the key to your cell and you sit and rot and—"

Tim grabbed my arm. "It's not worth it," he whispered in my ear.

"You're right, Tim. He's not worth it."

With a smile at me, Kevin said, "Let's go."

He led Evans to a group of uniformed police officers waiting for them at the end of the hallway.

Justice was finally served.

Lizzy came busting out the doors and hugged Tim and me. "I can't believe it. He's losing his license. Peggy told them everything. It's over. It's finally over."

I squealed and hugged her close. We headed back to Tim's house. "You can go back to work and you never need to worry about him again," I said.

She shook her head. "I can't go back there, Olivia. I can't. I need to start fresh."

I wanted to argue with her, but I knew she was right. I let out a sigh. How unfair that she was double victimized by those who refused to see her as the victim when she finally spoke up. She was the hero.

"What then? Where are you going??"

"I don't know, but right now I'm so relieved. No one will ever have to worry about Evans again. Even if the nurses all hate me, I don't care, Liv. He won't hurt them anymore, and he'll be behind bars for a while."

I knew how the court system worked. He would be given bail before we knew it, and he'd be out in no time, but I was not about to tell her that and ruin her moment. This was a big win either way.

Chapter 33

Lizzy

We went to Lyndsey and Kevin's house for a barbecue and it ended up being a celebration for Dr. Evan's arrest. Brad even blew up his mug shot and hung it up on the wall.

"I wish I could have been there to see the look on his face when Kevin put him in handcuffs," Maddy said.

"I love how you looked him right in the eyes and told him off. That was so great," Kat said to Olivia.

Olivia looked my way, and I flashed her a smile of respect and gratitude. She smiled back and sat down next to me at the table on the patio.

"Will you stay at the hospital or are you applying somewhere else?" she said.

Everyone looked at me. "I've been thinking about this for a while now and I've decided I'm going back to school to get my bachelor's degree."

"That's great, Lizzy," Troy said. "The opportunities are endless."

"What school?" Lyndsey said.

Tim got up and walked away.

"I'm planning on an online school so I can stick around here."

He stopped walking and turned around to look at me, a flash of surprise on his face.

"These past two years have been really hard without Aunt Victoria, and I didn't think I'd ever want to live here again. But the minute I returned and spent time with all of you again, I realized my heart will always be here. My aunt may be gone, but her spirit lives on."

"Agreed," Troy said. He glanced at Olivia. "Her memories live on with all of us. She'd be so proud of you, Lizzy. We all are."

"I know, and I think I may have given up on some other things a little too soon. I'm ready to stop running and choose happiness instead."

Tim looked at me. "Sometimes the heart wants what it wants."

Olivia squealed behind her hands. "Sorry, but you guys are talking about each other, aren't you? Are you back together?"

Tim lifted his eyebrow at me, and everyone looked from him to me.

"Well?" Brad said.

Lyndsey hit him on the shoulder and shushed him.

"What? I think we are all equally invested in this relationship, right?"

No one argued.

I had not planned on doing this right here, right now, but what the hell? I got up and walked over to Tim. I dropped to one knee, and he shook his head at me. "Two years ago, you got down on one knee and I turned you down because I wasn't ready. I was broken and hurt and stupid. It took some time for me to think about it, and I'm ready to stop running and open my heart for real this time."

He got down on one knee next to me. "I can't let you do this alone."

"Don't steal my moment," I said.

"I wouldn't dare. Go ahead, ask me."

"I'm getting there," I said in an annoyed tone. "Don't rush me."

He pursed his lips and tried not to let his smile peek through.

"I may not be good at this whole relationship thing, but if you can be patient with me, I promise I will do everything I can to stop running and start communicating."

He grabbed my hands and kissed me.

Everyone cheered, and Kevin whistled.

"Will you just say you'll marry me already?" I said in an annoyed tone.

He stood up, pulled me to my feet and then dipped me back and kissed me so intimately I felt like this was way too much for our friends to see, but they just clapped harder and cheered louder.

We walked out to the end of the dock after dark and sat down on the bench. A few raindrops sprinkled the dock. I did not care. Nothing would ruin this moment.

Tim held my hand in his lap and kissed me. I wrapped myself around his arm. "I can't believe we're engaged," I said.

"I can't believe you stole my moment," he said and kissed my cheek. "I need to ask you something."

We turned and looked into each other's eyes.

"It may be a weird time to bring this up, but I want to throw Olivia a baby shower and I was wondering if you would help me. I'm not great at these things, but I really want to do it for her."

"I love that you want to take the initiative. Usually, it's a woman who throws a baby shower, but I think it's sweet." I tucked my head under his chin and snuggled into him. "I would love to help."

The rain picked up and ran down my face and into my eyes.

Neither one of us moved.

I watched the rain drop into the lake and bounce off the top of the water in the moonlight.

He pulled me in closer. "Can I ask you another question?"

"Yeah," I whispered and pulled away to look at him as he spoke.

"Will you move in with me? When you are ready, of course," Tim said.

I nodded. "I want to have some time with Troy first, but I'd be honored. I can slowly start moving my two suitcases in."

He laughed.

"How many women only have two suitcases? I should feel like a lucky man to be with a woman that isn't high maintenance. I love that about you." He pushed my hair behind my shoulder.

My heart fluttered.

"You're so beautiful, and you aren't afraid to be who you are. That day on the dock when I met you, I needed to know more about you. You intrigued me."

"Same. I needed to see more of these abs," I said, poking him in the stomach.

He let out a grunt, then he kissed me.

We both stood up.

He took off his shirt and threw it on the bench.

We stared into each other's eyes, then I pulled my shirt over my head.

We undressed together, never breaking eye contact.

He took my face in his hands. His kiss was so deep it made my body warm.

He pulled away, smiled, and then jumped into the water. I followed, but Tim was not done yet. He pushed me against the boat and kissed me. His kisses trailed down my collarbone.

"I will never stop loving every inch of you, my sweet Lizzy."

I looked up at the sky and closed my eyes. For the last two years, I hadtried so hard to fight my feelings for him. Now, I was here with him in the water, making love to him in the most passionate sex I've ever shared with a man.

I never knew someone could make me feel this way. He opened up my heart and, for the first time, I did not fight my feelings for him this time. I wanted to make love to this man for the rest of my life. My body spasmed at his touch. The feel of his body against mine in the water was pure ecstasy. My senses heightened, and my body left satisfied. I never experienced anything like it, even with him before. This was what love felt like. I knew it deep in my soul.

Now he was mine, and I was the luckiest woman alive. I was going to marry this man, and the thought no longer made me nervous. I could notimagine life without him anymore.

Chapter 34

Olivia

I knew something was up when I saw the pink streamer dragging on the back of Lizzy's foot and then packages from Party Express arrived on Tim's front step. Maddy called and asked if I wanted to go to the Side Lake Rec Center with her and David and I knew my suspicions were correct.

The parking lot was full of familiar cars, including my sister Vivian's. My sister was so busy with her restaurant, but she was also the sister who always showed up when I needed her. We weren't as close as Tim and I were because we were just so different, but she was here. The rest of my sisters probably had not come.

"Olivia, it's been so long. Look at your cute baby bump," my sister said, touching my stomach. "I would never look as cute as you if I were pregnant. You're just glowing!"

I put my arms around her. "I'm so glad you're here, Viv. Where are the rest of the family?"

"You know how they are. They want to throw you a

shower in Duluth when it's a little closer, but I couldn't wait to see you. You couldn't keep me away."

"I'm so glad you came."

"I can't believe Tim threw you this shower. I can't get him to even come to the restaurant to fix the plumbing," she said, rolling her eyes.

"Have you ever asked him to?"

She laughed. "No, but I guess I should."

The sunny day was hot and humid. A typical day in July for Minnesota.

We played a couple games, including Baby Jeopardy, and we had to guess what candy bar was melted inside the diaper. I never laughed so hard. At one point, Kat's face turned green, and I thought she was going to vomit when she looked in the diaper full of melted Snickers.

I received so many gifts for the baby. How would I fit them all in Tim's house?

"I have to leave tomorrow, so I'd really like for you to come for a walk with me," my sister said.

The party was over, and the cleanup had begun. I wanted to stay and help clean but my friends shooed me out.

"Go spend some time with your sister," Lizzy said. "We've got this."

We decided to take a walk to McCarthy Beach, since it was only about a mile down the road. I wanted to take her to the beach so she could see how beautiful it was. My sister loved the sun and guys without shirts that took good care of their bodies.

She had a history of dating the wrong men, the bad boys with control issues and criminal histories. I never understood why. My sister was beautiful, smart, charismatic and funny, and also extremely successful. A real catch.

We started walking up the hill, the sun beating down on us.

"I can see why you and Tim like it here so much. It's such a cute community, but it's still not Duluth."

I laughed. Side Lake was a little too small town for my sister. "At one point I thought it was too rural for me, too, but it sure grew on me."

"Maybe."

"How's everything going? How's the restaurant?"

My sister grunted. "The restaurant is wonderful, but Zachariah and I broke up. It's been hard."

They'd been together a whole six months. Zac was one of her longer relationships, but I knew it was only a matter of time. She met him at the bar and hired him on to bartend, which was the first sign of failure for their relationship. He was handsome and charming, maybe too charming. He knew all the right things to say, and he was always disappearing and spent way too much time looking in the mirror.

"I'm sorry, Viv."

"Thanks, but it was a matter of time," she said, flipping her brown, naturally curly hair behind her ear and scrunching up the curls. "The biggest issue is he was really great at helping me run the bar and with our parents' never-ending health issues, I can't do it all by myself anymore."

"What's going on? Is mom having issues with her blood sugar again?" Their mother had type two diabetes and their father had problems with his ears and balance.

"Dad is struggling to take care of mom, but he gets really dizzy and the other day he fell."

I gasped. "Why didn't you tell me?"

"I'm telling you now, Liv. I need help. I can't do it on my own anymore. I talked to them about hiring a nurse to come in, but you know how they feel about hiring people to come into their home to help them. It's not going to happen and I'm just so worried about them."

My heart sank. "So you want me to move back to Duluth and help them?"

"You're the only one who has the flexibility. I had to try. You aren't due until Halloween, right? You're more than welcome to stay with me and drive over there or live with them until we can find out what's going on with dad."

"Viv, I just left there. I was looking forward to staying here with Tim. The lake is so peaceful."

I didn't plan on returning to the hospital after what happened to Lizzy. Although Dr. Evans was never coming back, if I went back there, it would be like stabbing Lizzy in the back, especially the way some nurses treated her. Some time would need to pass before they stopped talking about what happened.

"I'm not saying yes or no, but I need some time to think about it, okay?"

She squeezed my shoulder. "That's all I'm asking. Just think about it, okay?"

"I will."

"You didn't tell me how sexy your guy friends are. Are any of them single?"

I shook my head at her.

"What? I'm single."

"They're all taken," I said. "Their wives were all there. You met them."

"What about that guy with the cute dog? What was her name? Hope?"

"Troy," I said, a bit more defensive than I meant his name to come out.

She looked at me with a curious expression. "Wait a

minute. Is my sister having a fling with the ripped guy with the good hair?"

I shook my head. "No."

She gasped. "Liar! I know you, Liv. You're into him. Did you kiss him? Huh? Did you? Naughty girl."

"Nothing going on between us. He's just a friend."

"Your eyes tell me otherwise," she said.

We reached the beach and sat down in the sand. A few guys in their thirties were playing beach volleyball. Viv took all of five minutes before she joined in their game.

I laughed as I watched her. So carefree and outgoing. I knew our parents needed help, otherwise Viv would not have asked me to come home. She was a superwoman, and I always admired how she could run a thriving restaurant business, be on the city council, and always find time for Sunday brunch at our parents' house, plus visit them a couple times a week.

I had a feeling my parents were doing worse than Viv told me, and I needed to make a hard choice.

Chapter 35

Lizzy

Olivia knocked on my door close to nine o'clock.

"What are you doing here? Where's your sister?" I said. "She seemed really nice, and I immediately liked her."

"No, she went to The Viking for dinner with Tim. Troy called and asked me to come over. Is he here?"

My uncle appeared from behind me. "Hey Uncle Troy. Olivia is here."

"I actually invited her over," Troy said. "I have something to give you, and I wanted Olivia to be here. Get the key Victoria gave you."

My heart was about to beat out of my chest. "Wait, you figured out what the key was for?"

He nodded.

"Get the key and I'll meet you upstairs in my bedroom."

"Your bedroom?"

"Yes."

Uncle Troy was in his walk-in closet with a ladder. He climbed up and stuck his head in the attic.

"We're dying to find out what it is. Do you need some help up there, Uncle Troy?"

He sneezed. "It's so dusty up here. I think I can get it. Lizzy, why don't you climb halfway up the ladder, and I'll hand it to you.

"Okay."

I climbed up the ladder and popped my head inside the attic. I saw Troy as he sifted through boxes in the corner, then picked up a big chest and brought it over to me. I backed up and grabbed one side of the chest from Troy and slowly backed down the ladder with it. We set it down on the floor together.

Olivia led the way as Troy directed us to his room. Dust flew up from the chest as we walked.

"Ew." Olivia waved away the dust and coughed.

We wiped the beautiful wooden chest clean with a towel. The chest was finished and stained. Victoria's initials were engraved on a silver plate.

I looked at Troy and held my breath. Tears ran down my face at the anticipation. Olivia wiped them away with her thumb.

I put the key in the lock and it fit perfectly. I turned the key until the lock popped off. I hesitated, then took a deep breath and opened my aunt's treasure chest.

White fabric lay in the chest. I pulled it out and held up the dress. "Is this...?"

Troy nodded. "Victoria's wedding dress."

I forgot how beautiful it was. Their wedding at the lake flashed in my mind. The smile on her face as she came in on a boat. The most romantic and beautiful wedding I'd ever been to in my life.

"Is this for me? She gave this to me?"

He nodded. "Keep going," he said, his voice as excited as I felt.

I opened up a small jewelry box that held an elegant gold necklace with diamonds in the shape of an infinity symbol with a heart around it, a blue garter, a small diamond crown, and a gold wedding ring with diamonds in the same shape as the infinity symbol with a heart around it. "Oh, they're so beautiful."

"Keep going."

I picked up four white envelopes with writing on them. "Read now, Read on your wedding day, Give to Troy, and the last one is, To My Sister Diane on Lizzy's wedding day."

I handed Troy his letter, and he stared at it a minute before he folded it and put it under his leg. His envelope was the thickest of them all.

"I can't believe she did this," I said.

I put my finger under the seal, but Troy held up his hand and stopped me.

"Do you want Olivia and I to step out and give you some privacy while you read it? This is your moment?"

I wiped more tears from my face and shook my head. "I want you both here with me. Please."

Olivia put her arm around me and gave me a squeeze.

I opened up the letter and cleared my throat, but my voice came out nasally from the many tears I was shedding.

My Sweetest Niece,

I knew this day would come and you would find the person you were going to spend the rest of your life with. I have always thought of you as a daughter, and I could never be prouder of you and the person you have become as an adult.

Although I love my sister deeply, I know she really struggles with her maternal instincts and although she loves you very much, I knew I needed to be the one to give you away. As you have already seen, I have given you something old - my wedding ring and don't worry, Troy gave me his blessing because we both know you are the person we want to carry it forward. We love you so much and we knew you would find your partner once you were ready.

Something new is the necklace. I searched and searched to find the matching necklace to the earrings, but I ended up having them special ordered. They stand for forever. Just like the love Troy and I share, your love will last forever. Even on the hardest days of your marriage, don't stop fighting for your love. Marriage is hard work and dedication and, most of all, communication, and this necklace will help you remember that. The man you marry is your forever person and I'm so glad you found him. It is one of the best blessings in life. Never settle.

The earrings were borrowed from your grandmother on my wedding day. I never gave them back, but I know she will be more than happy that I gave them to you. And something blue, the blue garter. I had your initials and Tim's initials engraved on the heart. If you somehow don't end up marrying Tim, then I am very embarrassed right now and please just have the heart removed. But I know in my heart the connection you two share is hard to find, and I believe the two of you will be together forever. And the crown is because you need to feel like a princess on your special day and this is a reminder of how special you are.

If you haven't already done so, open up the box. Inside is my gift for you, so you don't have to start your marriage in debt. Have the wedding you want, whether it is small or big, whether you have the wedding of a lifetime or if you elope. Whatever money you have left, use it to go on the honeymoon of your dreams.

I really hate that I can't be there to give you away, but I will be right by your side as you walk down that aisle. My biggest advice to you is to make sure you are living your life for you because you will never be able to control what others think, only your reaction. Live your life and be kind. The true key to a happy marriage is lots of love, forgiveness, and compromise. I love you so very much, and whether you decide to wear my dress or buy a new one, is completely up to you. I want you to have the dress that made me the happiest woman as I held your uncle's hand and promised him my love forever.

Congratulations on this monumental moment and don't shed a tear for me, for I am right there with you every step of the way. I love you so much. Happy Happily Ever After.

Love you always,
Aunt Victoria

Troy and Olivia both had tears in their eyes. I hugged them both. The one item left in the chest was a large package. I opened it to reveal stacks of hundred-dollar bills held together by rubber bands. "Uncle Troy, did you know about this?"

He shook his head. "I knew about a few things she was giving you. When Olivia and I found the letter in the box downstairs that said your key opened the box at the highest level, I realized it had to be in the attic. She didn't want you to find the chest until you were ready to get married, so here we are."

"I can't believe it. Thank you so much."

I held the wedding dress in front of me again and put the ring on my finger. "It's so beautiful. Are you sure you're okay with me wearing it?"

Troy nodded. "I'd be more than honored. Congratulations."

Chapter 36

———

Olivia

We all met at Troy's house early the next afternoon for another barbecue. The kids were in the yard swinging on the new tree swing with Emma and the rest of us were on the deck overlooking the lake.

Vivian and I were in the kitchen, and she followed me out the sliding glass door to meet everyone. They were all having side conversations, and snacking on chips and dip and veggies.

I took a deep breath. "Hey guys. I want to talk to you about something important."

Tim and Maddy looked my way, but everyone else continued to chat.

"Is everything okay? You look upset," Maddy said.

"I have some news," I said, looking at Vivian to get her support. She squeezed my hand.

Maddy stood up on top of a nearby chair. "Guys, quiet. Liv needs to tell us something."

Everyone quieted.

"Hey guys," I said nervously. "The minute I moved in

with Tim, all of you were there for me. You were so kind and you let me be myself without judgement. I've never had that before."

I saw smiles all around.

Tim gave me an encouraging nod. He was the only one who knew what I was about to say.

"I've never had friends quite like you guys. You're more than friends, you're family, and I am so grateful for you." I pursed. This was so difficult. "But I've decided to move back to Duluth because my parents aren't in great health and I need to be there for them."

They groaned, sadness showed on their faces.

"Oh, sweetie," Maddy said. "I'm so sorry."

"It was a really hard decision, but I'm going to be their nurse for a while. I'm not sure how long I'll live there or what, but I think this is best for them, for me, and for the baby."

Kat hugged me, and all the women, including my sister, joined in a group hug. There wasn't a dry eye.

Once we broke apart, Troy looked at me. "When are you leaving?"

I could not read his expression.

"In a couple of minutes. My bags are packed and ready to go."

Troy's eyes widened. "I see."

The silence was uncomfortable.

"You're going to come back and visit, right?" Lizzy said.

"Of course. As much as I can. My dad has had some dizzy spells, so the doctors are trying to figure out what's going on. It may be nothing, but it could also be something very serious." I bit my lip.

"She's stepping up on behalf of our family," Tim said.

"I'm so proud of you, even if I really hate to see you go." He hugged me.

Troy turned away and walked down the stairs. I slipped away and followed him.

"Troy!"

He kept walking.

"Troy!" I said, louder this time.

I walked faster and grabbed onto his arm and spun him around. His eyes were filled with tears.

"Why didn't you tell me? Why did I find out this way? I know you don't owe me anything, but you didn't care enough to take me aside?"

My eyes teared up. "I knew if I told you before everyone else, I wouldn't be able to leave. I have to be there for my parents, Troy. I have no choice."

He nodded, struggling to look me in the eye.

"Ever since you showed up at the target range, I knew something was different about you. I laughed more. You gave me hope that maybe someday I could find someone. That kiss." He shook his head. "It meant something to me."

"It meant something to me, too," I said.

"I needed more time. I'm not ready for a relationship, but I want to be. I really like you, Liv. Even when you're sassy and rude. You're my friend."

"I know, and I feel the same way. The kiss we shared was real Troy. But look at me." I pointed to my stomach. "I'm having a baby and neither of us is in a place for a relationship right now. I don't want this to be the end of whatever this is between us, but I have to go. You can't come with me and I can't stay, so where does that leave us?"

He stared at me. Both of us knew I was right. We weren't ready for anything.

"I won't forget you, Troy. You're going to find yourself

an amazing partner one day. You're the perfect guy and I hate that I have to walk away, but I'll never forget you."

We moved closer. I wrapped my arms around him and squeezed him tight, breathing in the familiar scent of pine trees. "I hate how good you smell," I said.

His chest vibrated against mine as he laughed. His chest picked up pace, and I leaned back to look at him. He was in tears and now so was I, again.

We held each other tight until we both pulled away.

He looked into my eyes and he kissed me. The kiss was deep and passionate and what we both knew to be the last kiss we would share.

I pulled away, and he held my hands in his. "I will never forget you. Thank you for bringing me back to life."

I wiped my eyes and walked toward the car where my sister waited for me. She was staring at us with her eyes narrowed. She pursed her lips and got into the car.

Hope jumped up on me and I crouched down to rub her under her chin. "Take care of that daddy of yours, okay? I love you, girl."

As we drove away, I looked into the side mirror and saw him watching at us until we made a turn and he was no longer in sight.

Chapter 37

Lizzy

We were all out on the pontoon, enjoying the last few weeks of summer a month after Olivia left. We had struggled when she left, especially Troy. We could all see he had fallen for her, hard, but he was coming around.

"Hey, I'm going to ski," Troy said.

"Me, too," Tim said. "We'll run two ropes.

I held my breath in fear when it looked like they would run into each other or Troy's rope would choke Tim, but they were smarter than I thought. They skied flawlessly, and it was fun to watch.

Josh stopped the boat, and both Tim and Troy crawled into the boat. Josh cut the engine, and we floated in the middle of the lake, waving at boats as they passed by. Whitney had prepared sandwiches for everyone and passed them out.

"It's not the same without Olivia and Victoria, but I'm just so happy to have everyone still together," Kat said.

"It's not like Liv is that far away," Tim said. "And she's

getting quite the belly. Even if she was here, I doubt she'd want to go out boating."

"I can't believe you're going to be an uncle in like two months," Lyndsey said.

"That's a scary thought," Brad said.

Tim threw his towel and Brad caught it.

"Don't make me come over there and tackle you."

Tim stood up. "Bring it on."

He should have known better than to challenge Brad. He came running at Tim, picked him up, and threw him into the water. Kevin got up next and pushed Brad in. Pretty soon everyone was in the water except Josh.

"Quit being a wimp and get in the water," Whitney said.

"Someone has to make sure the boat doesn't float away," he said.

Tim, Troy, Kevin, and Brad all took turns jumping off the back of the boat and doing flips and cannonballs into the water, splashing all the women sitting at the back of the boat.

"You'd think you guys were too old to be so competitive," Lyndsey said.

"We're never too old to be competitive," Brad said.

Once everyone was back in the boat, Maddy held out her beer.

"I want to make a toast. Everyone hold out your drinks," she said.

We all did as she asked.

She sat up on her knees on the bench. "I feel so blessed to have every one of you in my life. What are the odds we would all end up in Side Lake and most of us living on Turtle Creek Road? I want to make a toast to every single one of you. For the friendships we've gained over the years and the hardships we've all been through together. I love you all so much and no matter where we are, near or far, we will always be the best of friends."

"That's right," Brad said. "Two of us may not be here, but they are always right here." He pounded on his chest with his fist.

"Here's to Victoria, Olivia, Ariel, and the friends of Turtle Creek Road and to many more years of sunshine, skiing, bonfires, and all of you."

We clinked cans in a group toast.

"To us," we said together.

* * *

Author's Note

This series has been one of my favorites to write. I love Side Lake and the magic of my childhood came to life as I wrote this series. I am excited to announce this is not the end of these characters. My next series will be a spinoff of Tim's five sisters, including a continuation of Olivia's story. Of course, the rest of Lizzy and Tim's story too. The friends of Turtle Creek Road aren't going anywhere and this isn't the end of Side Lake either.

First, I want to thank my amazing husband, Owen. He is a true real life Cinnamon Roll, and I am truly the luckiest woman alive. He's my person. I also have to thank my amazing daughter, Alexis, for all your help in listening to me read my story and helping me develop the story. I love you, girl.

Thank you to my amazing editor, Shirley Fedorak. Thank you for helping me make this book into what it has become. Thank you to Kristin Bryant for creating these beautiful covers and thank you to April Krampotich at Appletree for my author photos. Thank you to my beta readers for all your love and support, and thank you to my proofreaders. It really takes a village.

I had a dream of writing ten books, and I just have one to go to fulfill that dream. Thank you to you, the reader, for your love and support. Thanks for loving my characters and picking up this book. Thank you for spreading the word and supporting me on social media. Every one of you keeps me motivated on the hardest of days and I thank you so much.

Side Lake is a real place with beautiful beaches and friendly people. It is the place that inspires me and my books help me to escape from the challenges that are thrown my way in life.

If you would like to know more about upcoming book signings and be the first to know about the newest release, follow me on social media or sign up for my monthly newsletter and get a free copy of the first book I ever wrote, Always Right Here, for free.

To sign up for emails and receive a free book:
www.JenniferWaltersAuthor.com
Instagram:@JenniferWaltersAuthor
Facebook:@JenniferWaltersAuthorTikTok:
@JenniferWaltersAuthor

www.ingramcontent.com/pod-product-compliance
Lightning Source LLC
Chambersburg PA
CBHW020759310726
48969CB00002B/614